DECORATED
TO
DEATH

Books by Dean James

POSTED TO DEATH

FAKED TO DEATH

DECORATED TO DEATH

Published by Kensington Publishing Corp.

DECORATED TO DEATH

Dean James

KENSINGTON BOOKS
http://www.kensingtonbooks.com

KENSINGTON BOOKS are published by

Kensington Publishing Corp.
850 Third Avenue
New York, NY 10022

All Kensington Titles, Imprints, and Distributed Lines are available at special quantity discounts for bulk purchases for sales promotions, premiums, fund-raising, and educational or institutional use.

Special book excerpts or customized printings can also be created to fit specific needs. For details, write or phone the office of the Kensington special sales manager: Kensington Publishing Corp., 850 Third Avenue, New York, NY 10022, attn: Special Sales Department, Phone: 1-800-221-2647.

Kensington and the K logo Reg. U.S. Pat. & TM Off

ISBN 0-7582-0485-X

Library of Congress Control Number: 2003112538

First printing: April 2004
10 9 8 7 6 5 4 3 2 1

Printed in the United States of America

For Julie Herman,
whose friendship and support
never fail to sustain me

Acknowledgments

Thanks, as always, to my editor, John Scognamiglio, and the Kensington team for giving Simon and me such great covers and support; to my agent, Nancy Yost, for being so inimitably Nancy; to Megan Bladen-Blinkoff and Patricia Orr, who have given Simon and me unstinting encouragement and friendship; to Betty Rowlands, for help with certain matters of technology; and, finally, to Tejas Englesmith, who is the difference that makes each and every thing better and brighter.

Chapter One

Dead people hate housework just like everybody else. Otherwise a vampire like me wouldn't have let a stranger have the run of Laurel Cottage twice weekly. I don't keep a coffin hidden somewhere on the premises—there's no longer any need to hide in one during the day, thanks to some lovely little pills—but I nevertheless felt a bit nervous hiring a strange person to come in to clean.

Violet Glubb seemed perfectly ordinary in most respects. Other than her unfortunate name, that is. She was reasonably attractive, if one liked the type. Women, that is. I don't, at least not in that way.

Violet had a pretty face and a fair figure and was about twenty-five or thereabouts. If she were older, she concealed it well enough behind a facade of youthful exuberance and a limited vocabulary. She also seemed very much to want the job, expressing her willingness to keep Laurel Cottage in order for the not-so-modest sum I was offering. Since any other charpersons in Snupperton Mumsley, the Bedfordshire village I now called home, had thus far neglected to express the least interest in the advertisement I had posted in the village shop-cum-post office over a week ago, the job was Violet's for the taking.

She accepted the job, shaking my hand with great vigor and smiling up at me with sparkling enthusiasm in her eyes. Evidently she loved to clean; indeed, she lived to clean, if she were to be believed. I was her second client in Snupperton Mumsley, her first being Jessamy Cholmondley-Pease, the wife of one of our local councillors. She had time for at least another one or two, however.

"You might check with Lady Prunella Blitherington at Blitherington Hall, Miss Glubb," I said. I wouldn't normally wish such a fate on anyone, but Violet Glubb seemed capable enough to face even a harridan like Lady Prunella.

She interrupted with a giggle, "Nobuddy calls me that, Mr. Kirby-Jones, just plain Vi will do."

"Ah, yes . . . Vi," I said, wincing at her high-pitched amusement, "Anyway, Lady Blitherington often seems in need of assistance at the Hall."

She giggled again. "I heard tell of her, Mr. K.-J., down at the pub. They do say she be a right battle-ax."

We both turned at the sound of a loud guffaw emanating from the doorway of the sitting room. My assistant, Giles Blitherington, stood there clutching his sides in mirth. Whether he was laughing at my new nickname or the all-too-apt description of his mother remained to be discerned.

"Giles Blitherington, may I present Miss Violet Glubb, my new cleaner. Vi, Giles Blitherington, my assistant."

Having gained control of his amusement, Giles advanced into the room and offered his hand politely to Violet. "How do you do, Miss Glubb? It's indeed a pleasure." He offered her one of his killer smiles, and I could see Vi starting to melt right in front of him.

Giles is a handsome devil, and he knows it, but his

charm is such a natural part of his character that it's effortless. He is no more interested in women than I am; he's rather more interested in Yours Truly, which he makes known as frequently as he believes he can get away with it. I have thus far resisted his blandishments, because I've no idea how he'll react when—or should I say, if—he discovers that I am one of the living dead.

I cleared my throat, and Violet turned her attention back to me. "Giles assists me with my research and writing, Violet. He keeps my work existence organized. I am counting on you to help me keep the rest of my existence clean and tidy."

She giggled again. I supposed I would eventually grow used to it, but giggling females were not high on my list of Things I Can Abide. Especially since the frequency of giggles seemed inversely proportional to IQ levels, and Violet's IQ was dropping rapidly.

"They told me down at the pub you was a writing gentleman, Mr. Kayjay. I don't read much, meself, unless it's Barbara Cartland. She writes such grand love stories, dun't she?" She sighed rapturously, remembering, I supposed, one of those grand Cartlandian tales. I tried not to shudder.

"If you like love stories, Vi," Giles said, throwing a wicked grin in my direction, "I'm sure Mr. Kayjay will give you a copy of one of his favorites by Daphne Deepwood. I've heard she writes really grand love stories, too, though I've not read them."

Violet's eyes grew big. "Really, Mr. Kayjay? That'd be a fair treat, that would."

I arched an eyebrow in Giles's direction. "Yes, Vi, I might have a spare copy in my office." Since I *am* Daphne Deepwood, and well Giles knows it, I did have more than a spare copy or two in my office. But if Barbara Cartland were Violet's idea of a grand love story, she might find one of my historical romances a bit too long and complicated for her taste. Far be it from me, however, to disdain a potential fan.

While Giles entertained Violet, I went to my office to find a copy of the latest Daphne Deepwood offering, *Passion in Peru,* which was still riding high on the bestseller list. I took great satisfaction in seeing the rows of my books upon the shelves. Daphne Deepwood had penned five books thus far, and number six was in the works. As Dorinda Darlington I had published four private-eye novels, featuring a tough female shamus. Under my own name I had published two well-received biographies of medieval queens.

One of the advantages of being dead was that I required little sleep, and I spent a lot of time writing. I was even thinking of launching a new pseudonym, under which I would write cozy English village mysteries. At the rate I was stumbling over dead bodies since settling in Snupperton Mumsley, I figured I might as well make good use of my own misadventures in sleuthing.

Violet accepted the copy of *Passion in Peru* happily, and I asked Giles to show her through Laurel Cottage. "If you need anything in the way of cleaning supplies and so on, Vi, just let Giles know. He will give you money, or purchase them himself for you. Whichever works best for you."

"Ta, Mr. Kayjay," Violet beamed at me. "I can get things at the shop on my way here, if need be. It's right on me way."

"Very well," I said. "Then we're agreed, Tuesday and Friday afternoons?"

Violet nodded. "I'll be back tomorrow, Mr. Kayjay."

"Off you go then," I said, smiling as she prepared to follow Giles around the cottage. I retreated to my office and shut the door. I was about halfway through the latest

Deepwood opus and determined not to slack off, as I am occasionally wont to do during the mid-book doldrums.

I was deep into a mad chase on horseback through the Kent countryside when Giles broke through my concentration. I turned to scowl at him.

"Sorry, Simon," Giles said, backing off a bit. I can appear quite fierce without meaning to, and from the look on Giles's face, I had evidently made him a bit nervous.

"What is it, Giles?" I tried not to sound annoyed.

"I wouldn't interrupt you when you're working like that, Simon," Giles said, reproach in his voice, and I relented, giving him a brief, conciliatory smile, "but you did say to remind you about getting ready for the big event this afternoon."

"What?" I frowned, trying to recall the event to which he referred.

Giles shook his head. "Honestly, Simon, if I weren't here to keep you organized, what would you do?" He approached my desk, pushed my desk calendar towards me, and pointed. I peered at it. "Lady B. Tea. Harwood etc." I read that aloud, then groaned.

"Yes, Simon, I know. I know you detest tea at the manor, but this ought to be interesting." Giles laughed in wicked glee. "Remember who the guest of honor is?"

Comprehension dawned, as my brain finally cleared of Kentish fog. "Ah, yes, the King of Home Decorating. Hezekiah Call-Me-Zeke Harwood." I laughed. "Or should I say the Queen of Home Decorating?"

"The one and only," Giles said, smiling. "And given the bitchy comments you've made about him, surely you wouldn't want to miss a minute of the festivities."

"No," I said, standing up and stretching. Even my neck and shoulders get cramped from hunching too long over a computer screen. "I imagine he's even more outrageous in person than he is on television. And some of the travesties he's wreaked upon those poor folk who've agreed to let him redecorate their homes for his program!"

Laughing, Giles said, "Then we'll expect you at Blithering-ton Hall in about an hour. I'm off to see whether Mummy needs help with any last-minute arrangements."

"I'll be there," I replied, gazing at my computer screen. There was something about that chase scene that wasn't quite right. Perhaps just a few more minutes.

"No, Simon," Giles said. "Save the file, and turn it off. If you sit back down there, we'll never see you. And Mummy would be *so* disappointed if you're not there."

Relieved would be more like it, I thought. Giles's mother and I had an uneasy relationship. She resented my giving him a job, which she considered beneath his dignity as "Sir" Giles, Lord of the Manor, and she also feared I had designs on what remained of his virtue. If she only knew that it was he who had designs on mine, the poor dear would no doubt faint dead away.

"Right you are, Giles," I said, sighing. I'd leave Marianna and Charles dashing along through Kent for a while yet. They would keep.

I followed Giles to the front door. "Do you think Violet will work out?"

Giles paused in the act of pulling on his jacket. He grinned. "She's taken quite a shine to you, Simon. All the while I was showing her around the cottage, she kept talk-ing about how distinguished and handsome you are, Mr. Kayjay." He mimicked her voice and her giggle so well I couldn't suppress a shudder of distaste.

"I could always tell her, Simon, that you're spoken for. And by whom."

He never lets up, and it wouldn't do to let him realize that I've begun to weaken, ever so slightly. I gave him The Look, as he called it. The one that was supposed to quell him, but which had begun to lose its effect lately.

"Well, then, Simon, I'll be off. See you in a while." Not cowed in the least, he winked before opening the door and heading for his car. I watched him walk away, enjoying the view, then shut the door and leaned back against it.

All I needed was a moonstruck cleaning lady *and* Giles competing for my romantic attentions. Times like this I almost wished I did have a coffin to which to retire during the day. So much for the old days, I thought, as I headed upstairs for one of the magic little pills that makes my existence as a vampire free of the need for blood.

Trusting that I had timed it right, I arrived at Blitherington Hall some two hours after Giles had left Laurel Cottage. Figuring that a television celebrity of the magnitude of Zeke Harwood would not deign to arrive on time, I had lingered at home, jotting down notes for the village mystery I was contemplating writing. By the time I arrived there were several cars in the forecourt of the Hall, and I parked the Jaguar behind the tatty Golf belonging to the vicar and his wife.

Giles had managed to talk his mother out of a garden party, with the whole village in attendance, persuading her that a more intimate tea would be the proper event with which to welcome a television celebrity and his entourage. Not to mention that it was far less expensive. I was thankful not to have to bring along sunglasses and a hat to ward off the sun, made necessary by attendance at an outdoor function. Those pills I take make it possible for me to go about in the daytime, as long as I take sensible precautions against the sun. But it's much easier in the fall, when the sun heads down quite soon in the afternoon. The brisk temperature outside is quite refreshing; to me, at least. I think I might have enjoyed the garden party more. At least there would have been more people between me and dear Lady Prunella.

I clanged the ornate door knocker up and down a few times and waited. Finally the door opened, and I stepped inside.

"Good evening, Thompson," I said. "How are you this evening?"

"Tolerable, Professor, tolerable," the venerable butler responded in his raspy voice. A rather unprepossessing specimen, and eighty if he was a day, Thompson wavered on thin legs, blinking at me. He should have been retired long ago, but Lady Prunella was far too cheap to pension him off. She could never afford to replace him, because no one in his right mind would have worked for her the past thirty-five years with the devotion that Thompson had displayed.

"If you'll follow me, sir," Thompson said, tottering off in the direction of the drawing room.

"You needn't announce me, Thompson," I said, halting him before he had gone more than a few steps. I hated to see the poor old thing run back and forth like this, when he ought to be resting somewhere with his feet up and a nice tot of whiskey at hand for relaxation.

Thompson stopped and turned around. "As you wish, Professor. I'm sure you know the way."

"Certainly, Thompson." I smiled at him, and his lips twitched in response. He lurched back toward the front door to await the next arrival, and I strode on to the drawing room.

The buzz of several conversations assailed me as I opened the door. There were about fifteen people in the room, including Giles and Lady Prunella, one of our local councillors and his wife, and the vicar and his good lady. Lady Prunella was engrossed in delivering some sort of mini-tirade to the councillor and thus too busy to notice me, and I sidled up to the vicar, Neville Butler-Melville, and his wife, Letty, who stood sipping their tea on the side of the room well away from our hostess.

They welcomed me with warm smiles. I had worried, after the nasty murder which occurred right after I had settled in Snupperton Mumsley, that they would rather have nothing further to do with me.* Fortunately they held nothing against me, and we had become much better acquainted since then.

"What a lovely hat, Letty," I lied. Poor Letty hadn't the fashion sense God gave a duck, but she did try, however misguided her efforts. I figured I might as well encourage her. Neville was so devoted to her, he never realized how ridiculous she looked. The concoction of feathers and fruit she sported atop her head looked like parakeets having an orgy in the produce section, but it was colorful, if nothing else.

Letty flushed with pleasure, and Neville beamed with pride. Neville was scrumptious in his clerical kit, as ever the handsome poster boy for the Anglican Church.

"How's the latest book going, Simon?" Neville asked. "Didn't you tell me you were working on a study of medieval queenship?"

"Yes, Neville, that's right, and it's going well, if slowly." Only Giles among the locals knew that I wrote popular fiction, and I was working on a scholarly book, in between stints on romances and mysteries. At the rate I was going, the scholarly book wouldn't be finished for another two years, at least.

Before Neville could launch into a series of tedious questions—he fancied himself as quite the amateur historian—I changed the subject with ruthless speed. "Isn't it exciting to think of our having such a celebrity in our midst for the next week?"

"Oh, yes, Simon," Letty replied with great enthusiasm. "I shouldn't confess to indulging in something so frivolous, but I do so enjoy watching Mr. Harwood's program,

*Author's note: Kindly consult *Posted to Death* for further details.

"Très Zeke." Such a clever name, don't you think? I've taken some of his ideas and adapted them for use in doing some redecorating at the vicarage. And with, though I say it myself, quite lovely results."

As Neville beamed approvingly upon his wife, I kept a polite smile plastered on my face. I had seen Letty's "adaptations," and they were no more successful than Letty's attempts to dress herself with some sense of style or taste.

"Of course," Letty continued a bit wistfully, "if one had the budget most of Mr. Harwood's clients seem to possess, it would all go so much more easily, I'm sure."

"No doubt," I said. Most of the persons who appeared on Harwood's program were already well-heeled, or they couldn't have afforded the hideously extravagant paints and fabrics that Harwood never failed to choose for his work. The program footed half the cost of the redecorating, but it was still an expensive proposition for those lucky enough to be chosen for the program. "I wonder when the man of the hour will deign to appear?"

Before either Neville or Letty could reply to the sarcasm-laden question, a hush fell over the room. We turned to see what had occasioned the quiet.

A few steps inside the doorway, accompanied by four people, there stood a man of average height, going bald at the front, dressed in a purple suit with a pink shirt. Ignoring the people awaiting him, he surveyed the room, his lip curling upward in disgust.

"What a dump."

Chapter Two

───────◆───────

Both Bette Davis and Elizabeth Taylor had delivered the line with more conviction, and certainly more panache, but Zeke Harwood managed to inject at least as much venom into the famous words as the two great actresses.

Like any queen, he knew how to make an entrance. One could have heard the proverbial pin drop for a long moment after he uttered those words.

Then someone giggled, and I recognized the sound. Jessamy Cholmondley-Pease, wife of the councillor and walking fashion faux pas, shut up abruptly when she realized all eyes had turned to her. Her face, raccoon-like with its injudicious use of kohl and eye shadow, suffused with red as she tried to shrink behind her husband. Thanks to the ridiculously high spiked heels she wore, her bottle-blond head stuck up over her husband's silvery dome, making them look like some bizarre totem pole.

"Which of you unfortunates is the lady of the manor?" Zeke Harwood's voice, nasal and high-pitched, reclaimed our attention.

Even Lady Prunella Blitherington, rarely at a loss for words, was struck dumb by this further bit of colossal rudeness. Having seen the man's program on a few occasions, I knew he had all the tact of a runaway bulldozer, but I had figured it was just his "Très Zeke" persona. Evidently not.

Giles recovered first. Stepping forward, he went to greet the guest of honor. "How do you do, Mr. Harwood? I am Sir Giles Blitherington. May I present my mother, Lady Prunella Blitherington?" Lady Prunella stumbled forward, her face displaying her confusion. Should she snub this worm, or ignore his behavior?

"How do you do, Lady Prudence?" Harwood purred at her. "I see you are in desperate need of my services. How fortunate that you wrote in to my little program." He patted Lady Prunella's hand. "Yes, I see we'll have quite a lot of work to do here."

Lady Prunella said not a word. Her mouth hung open, but nothing issued forth.

Turning back to Giles, Harwood leered up into his face. "I see that at least one thing here at the manor needs no redecorating. How scrumptious."

Stone-faced, Giles stared back at him. Jessamy Cholmondley-Pease tittered again, but a quick elbow in the stomach from her husband shut her up.

"Perhaps, Mr. Harwood," Giles said in a tone that would have frozen boiling water, "you would like to introduce your companions."

Harwood blinked. Giles had not acted according to pattern, and he appeared confused. He clamped his mouth shut, raised a hand, and gestured with two fingers.

One of Harwood's companions, a tall, lanky man in his fifties, stepped forward.

"How do you do, Sir Giles?" His tone was polite and unctuous. "If I might, I'll introduce myself. I am Piers Limpley, Mr. Harwood's personal assistant." He towered over his employer, who had stepped a few paces back and stood glowering at Giles and the rest of us.

"A pleasure, Mr. Limpley," Giles said, his tone thawing noticeably as he shook hands.

"Sir Giles, Lady Prunella, if I might introduce the rest of Mr. Harwood's staff." He indicated the young woman standing next to him. "Dittany Harwood, Mr. Harwood's sister, and the designer and webmaster of his Web site."

The thirtyish Dittany had a strong resemblance to her brother, the same mulish chin and short hair already going gray, but her posture spoke volumes. She was doing her best to fade into the background, trying not to be noticed. She managed to mumble a greeting to us, then retreated behind Piers Limpley.

"And this is Moira Rhys-Morgan, Mr. Harwood's housekeeper." The stately redhead offered a polite nod in our direction. Like Dittany Harwood, she was wearing a sensible dark business suit. The gaze she directed toward her employer held affection mingled with exasperation. Interesting.

Limpley had saved the best for last. He gestured toward a stunningly handsome man in his late thirties. I had been trying not to stare at him, although I had noticed that Giles was not suffering from any shyness in doing so. "This is Cliff Weatherstone, the producer of Mr. Harwood's program."

"How do you do?" A voice like warm honey oozed into our ears, and I would have sworn that I heard Lady Prunella gasp before she simpered and took his proffered hand.

After Lady Prunella released him, with obvious reluctance, Weatherstone extended his hand to Giles. Giles, too, seemed to linger over the handshake. Was it my imagination, or was Weatherstone giving Giles a discreet cruise?

Zeke Harwood had been watching the two handsome younger men with eyes narrowed. He stepped forward and laid a possessive hand on Weatherstone's arm. "Cliffie darling, you mustn't monopolize our handsome host."

Weatherstone's face flushed in annoyance, and he did his best to shrug off Harwood's hand without seeming to do so. Giles fixed Harwood with a most unfriendly look, then pointedly turned away from him.

"Might I introduce you to our friends?" Giles said, motioning me to come forward. "Dr. Simon Kirby-Jones, an eminent American historian recently come to Snupperton Mumsley." I nodded in the general direction of the Harwood posse. Cliff Weatherstone offered me a warm smile while the rest blinked or nodded.

"Our vicar, Neville Butler-Melville and his lady wife, Letty." More nods and blinks, on both sides.

"Our esteemed councillor"—was there the merest touch of irony in Giles's voice?—"Desmond Cholmondley-Pease and his wife, Jessamy."

Jessamy, unlike the rest of us, tottered forward on her high heels in order to grasp Harwood's hand. Ridiculous shoes to wear for such a gathering, I reflected. Pretty ridiculous to wear for any purpose, as far as I was concerned, but in my limited acquaintance, Jessamy Cholmondley-Pease never dressed appropriately for anything. Unless it were for a prostitutes' convention. Her makeup always looked like she had troweled it on, and she probably had every variation of garment ever made from faux-leopard print material. It was her signature fabric, or so I had heard her airily informing someone in the post office just last week.

"Oh, Mr. Harwood, I watch "Très Zeke" all the time. It's ever so clever, how you work wonders with everyone's houses. I've watched your program so much I feel that I know you, or that we've even met before." She laughed. "I only wish we could have you at our home to work one of your miracles." She threw a spiteful glance at Lady Prunella. "But I guess we're not as posh as some I could name."

Harwood suffered her to hold his hand for a moment, then slowly pulled it away. "A very interesting name, Jessamy." He tittered. "Madam, if I were you, I'd be more concerned about taking legal action against my couturier than worrying about redecorating my house."

Now, our Jessamy might be more than a few bricks short of a full load, but even she couldn't mistake that insult for what it was. Her screech of rage startled us all, even though I could feel the hatred emanating from her in a sudden burst. She moved in Harwood's direction, but her husband, the long-suffering Desmond, was quicker. He has had many years of practice, I presume, in keeping rein over dear Jessamy's temper. He had her away from Harwood and into a corner of the room before most of us realized what almost happened.

Harwood turned with a smirk to Giles, but that smirk faded quickly at the look of distaste and contempt Giles failed to mask.

With a petulant toss of his head, Harwood turned back to his assistant, Piers Limpley. "I simply must rest now, Piers. This has been a frightfully long day, and I must have time to let my inspiration build for the task that awaits us. I'd like to be taken to my rooms now."

"Yes, of course, Zeke," Limpley said, his tone void of any inflection. "Sir Giles, if you wouldn't mind?"

"Certainly, Mr. Limpley," Giles said. "If you and Mr. Harwood and the rest would follow me, I shall show you to your rooms. Thompson, the butler, will see to your luggage." He strode forward, with Harwood and the others trailing behind him. "I presume you were able to find suitable accommodation for your crew in the village, Mr. Weatherstone?"

Weatherstone's assurances floated back to us as we watched them disappear through the door.

"A most unpleasant man," Neville Butler-Melville observed, shaking his head. "And a great disappointment, I fear, my dear Letty."

Letty did appear crestfallen, but she responded gamely to her husband's concern. "I expect he is very tired, Neville dear. None of us appear at our best when we are tired, do we?"

There was the slightest hint of reproach in her voice, as Letty very properly, at least in her view, turned the other cheek.

The guests began moving forward to bid farewell to their hostess. After all, there seemed little point in remaining. I waited until everyone else had taken leave of Lady Prunella before moving forward to grasp her hand in mine.

"My dear Lady Prunella," I said, "how unfortunate that someone of your breeding should be the victim of such an outrageously vulgar and common display." I oozed sympathy, and Lady Prunella responded with a trembling smile.

"Thank you, Dr. Kirby-Jones. At least some among us do have manners." Her lips narrowed into a thin line. "I fear I shall come to regret ever inviting that . . . that *toad* into my home!"

I patted her hand, then released it. "Perhaps dear Letty was correct, and Mr. Harwood will be much improved after a night's rest."

Lady Prunella emitted a most unladylike snort. "Chance would be a fine thing!"

"I wouldn't lay odds against you."

"I shall have to rely on Giles to deal with that man," Lady Prunella said, her voice softening. "The dear boy has demonstrated the most astonishing maturity in recent months." Her eyes caught mine briefly, then danced away. "A most delightful change."

For the moment, that was the closest she would come to

saying that I had actually been a positive influence in her son's life. To my own surprise, I felt a spurt of burgeoning respect for her.

"Yes, he is growing up," I said, smiling.

"Still, I cannot expect Giles to shoulder all the burden of dealing with that horrible man." She shuddered. "How ever will we get through the next week?"

"I believe, dear lady, that it is now out of your hands, so to speak. You must resign yourself to playing hostess, with the knowledge that he and his retainers will be gone in a few days. After all, how bad can it be?"

Lady Prunella took some comfort from my words, but I should have known better than to tempt fate in such fashion.

Chapter Three

Just before lunchtime the next day Giles regaled me with tidbits from the further adventures of Zeke Harwood at Blitherington Hall. I had been writing feverishly since about three that morning, and when Giles arrived at nine, I was far too deep into the misadventures of Marianna and Charles in the wilds of Kent to want to be diverted by anything mundane. But along about noon the pace slowed, and I limped to a halt, mentally worn out by what I had accomplished in my marathon writing bout. By that time I was more than ready to relax with a cup of tea and some gossip.

"The worst moment came, Simon, when Zeke insisted upon taking the master bedroom for himself. I thought Mummy would pop off from an apoplexy right then and there."

"It's not a particularly comfortable room," I said. "Why your mother insists upon keeping it for herself when one of the other suites of rooms would be far nicer, I don't know."

"Because it's the *master* bedroom, silly man," Giles said in mock-exasperation. "Mummy still fancies herself as the master of Blitherington Hall, naturally. And most of the time, I let her have her way, because it gives her more than enough to do and keeps her out of my way. I don't want that room. You're right. It's uncomfortable, and it would cost a tidy little packet, which I haven't got, to make it into something decent."

I laughed. "Maybe you should have Zeke and his crew redo that room, instead of the drawing room."

Giles snorted. "It's going to be bad enough, watching him wreak havoc downstairs. Whatever possessed Mummy to write into that program? I suppose she wanted something new and different."

I arched one eyebrow and stared at him for a moment. "Not unlike you with a certain gorgeous television producer last night, if my eyes weren't deceiving me. Tell me, how is your friend Cliff this morning?"

Giles's mouth dropped open, but he made a quick recovery. "I don't bloody believe it, Simon. You're actually jealous. You, jealous of Cliff Weatherstone." He crowed with laughter.

Were I still human, no doubt my face would have reddened with annoyance. "Nonsense, Giles, nothing could be further from the truth. I was merely noting what I had observed, but obviously I cannot stop you from misinterpreting my comments."

Eyes rolling, Giles said, "Oh, excuse me, Simon, excuse me."

Deciding to ignore his juvenile behavior, I reverted to the initial subject of our conversation. "What was the outcome, then, of Harwood's request for the master bedroom?"

"What? Oh, you might know, Mummy gave in. She wasn't about to indulge in vulgar fishwife antics and tell the bloody man there was no way in hell she was going to let him have the room. So Mummy stiffened her upper lip and let

Harwood have his way. After all, it's only for a few days, and we have more than enough rooms to accommodate them all."

I decided I might as well be blunt about one thing. "Who's paying for all this redecorating? Your mother is such a pinch-penny, I can't believe she's willing to pay for it all."

Giles grinned. "Oh, no flies on Mummy, rest assured. Before she wrote to the program, suggesting Blitherington Hall for a remake, she ascertained that the program pays for half of everything, and she has the opportunity to say no to anything too extravagant. If we hate what Harwood does, however, we bear the cost of changing it. But that's the worst of it. It's going to cost a mint to feed them all for several days, not to mention having to hire a few extra staff to clean the rooms, and so on. But Harwood's toady, Piers Limpley, assured me that they would cover the costs of that as well."

"What are you doing about extra staff, then?" Lady Prunella was legendary for running off staff after only a brief stint of work at Blitherington Hall.

"The one advantage of having these television people in the house is that suddenly we have quite a few villagers willing to work for a few days at the Hall. Women who practically laughed in Mummy's face in days gone by are now quite desperate to 'help out' there." He snickered. "Jessamy Cholmondley-Pease even volunteered. She seems rather fascinated by our celebrity and his minions, I must say."

"Hoping she'll be discovered, no doubt, along with all the others. Or perhaps they all just want to get Harwood's autograph, is that it?" The disgust was evident in my voice.

"Something like that," Giles said. "But we won't lack for staff the next few days, and at bargain rates, no less."

"You're a sharp operator, Giles," I said, not meaning it entirely as a compliment.

"Perhaps, Simon," Giles responded, his tone the tiniest bit huffy, "but if you'd care to trade places with me for a few days, you'd be more than welcome."

"No, thank you," I said. "I quite see your point." I smiled in conciliatory fashion.

"If it weren't for the fact that I need to keep an eye on Zeke and his minions, I might beg you to let me stay here with you until this bloody television program is over and done with."

"I'm sure Cliff Weatherstone would be most disappointed," I said.

"No doubt," Giles said, his eyes narrowing. "He at least is forthright about what he wants."

Before I could muster a response to that, the doorbell rang, followed by the sound of a door opening.

"Hello there!" A voice called. "Are ya there, Mr. Kayjay? It's me, Vi Glubb."

Giles made it into the hall to greet Violet ahead of me. I found her beaming up at Giles with the same kind of entranced look he had received from Cliff Weatherstone last night. Upon sight of me, however, she transferred that adoring gaze to Yours Truly.

Maybe Violet couldn't help it and anything male in pants got the same treatment. Hoping I wasn't going to regret hiring her, I said, "Welcome back to Laurel Cottage, Vi, and good Tuesday morning to you. Ready to start whipping the place into shape?"

"Go on with you, Mr. Kayjay," she said, giggling. I winced. "I don't expect as I'll be having all that much to do, for you looks like a proper tidy gentleman. Not like some, I could tell you."

I decided I'd better forestall her before she did tell me all about the Cholmondley-Peases, and at great length. "Nevertheless, Vi, I'm sure the place could use a good and thorough cleaning. Every room except my office, that is. I'd prefer not to have anything done in there. Giles and I between us will see that it's kept tidy." I smiled. "As tidy, that is, as it can ever be."

Violet giggled again. "Whatever you say, Mr. Kayjay, whatever you say. Now, has you had your lunch yet? You want I should make something up for you? And you too, Sir G.?"

"No, thank you, Vi," I said, hastily. "I'm a light eater, and I don't require anything for lunch."

"Go on, Mr. Kayjay, a big man like you must have quite an appetite." She giggled again and actually batted her eyelashes at me. I wondered what kind of appetite she was referring to, but I decided I had better pretend ignorance.

"A hearty breakfast, Vi," I said, matching my tone to the words, "that's the ticket. Sticks to my ribs and lasts me most of the day. No need for much else during the day."

"Whatever you say, Mr. Kayjay," Violet repeated. "What about you, Sir G.?"

"Thank you for the kind offer, Vi," Giles said, carefully not looking in my direction, "but I have other plans for lunch today. I'm meeting a friend in the village."

From the way Giles was acting, I decided I knew the identity of this friend. Cliff Weatherstone, to be sure. No doubt they had much to discuss about the use of Blitherington Hall for the filming of Harwood's program.

And the queen was planning to ask Parliament to abolish the monarchy.

"Until time for your appointment, Giles," I said sweetly, "perhaps you wouldn't mind focusing on the job I pay you rather handsomely to perform?" I ignored his expression of outrage and turned to Violet. "I just realized, Vi, that you are quite a bit early today. I thought we had agreed upon afternoons, had we not?"

Giles stomped off while Violet glanced uncertainly back and forth between us. "Sorry, sir," she said, more subdued than I had yet seen her. "I can go and come back later, if that's what you'd like. But I thought, this being my first day and all, I might come a bit early and give everything a good going over."

"That's quite all right," I assured her. "Have at it, and if you need anything, I'll be in my office, and Sir G. will be in his."

Violet ducked her head and loosed a nervous giggle. "Sure thing, Mr. Kayjay. I'll be so quiet, you won't even know as I'm here."

So saying, she headed for the kitchen at the back of the cottage, and I went back to my office and sat down behind the desk. I stared at the computer screen. I was now in a foul mood, and trying to write when I'm like this is impossible.

I roused from my unprofitable thoughts when I heard the sound of a throat being cleared. I looked up.

Giles stood there, a frown marring his handsome face. "If it's all the same to you, Simon, I think I might take the rest of the day off. I've really nothing very pressing at the moment here, and there are a number of matters I should be attending to at home and in the village. So, with your leave?" He turned to go, as if my acquiescence were a foregone conclusion.

"Go right ahead," I said. "I'll get along just fine without you this afternoon."

From the set of his shoulders, I guessed that Giles was doing his best to keep his temper with me. "I'm sure you will, Simon," he said in an odd tone. "I'll see you tomorrow."

The door closed behind him with a distinct "thump" moments later. *Well,* I thought, *that was certainly odd.* What had gotten into him?

I mulled it over for a moment, then grimaced. If Giles thought I was going to make a fuss and insist that he stay here with me the rest of the day, he had been sorely disappointed. If he wanted to play little games with his handsome television producer, he could go right ahead. I had no time for such silliness. I had more than enough work to do, with or without him.

Back to Marianna and Charles, I decided. I had only a couple of chapters to go, and the latest opus by Daphne Deepwood would be done.

I worked steadily for another couple of hours, my fingers flying over the keyboard, as I did my best to get Marianna and Charles together by the requisite point. For some reason, however, it just wasn't working. Finally, I hit the command to save what I had done and powered the computer down in disgust.

I headed up the stairs to freshen up and change clothes. Perhaps a stroll through the village might lighten my mood. I hadn't visited the local bookshop for several days, and there might be something new to tempt me there.

As I reached the head of the stairs, I saw Violet coming out of the bathroom wearing rubber gloves and toting a bucket full of cleaning supplies. She gave a start upon seeing me.

"Blimey, Mr. Kayjay, you do give a body a surprise, creeping about like a cat." She clutched one gloved hand over her heart, and her face flushed with a touch of red.

"Sorry, Vi, didn't mean to startle you," I said. She seemed a bit more nervous than the situation warranted, but perhaps she was one of those people who startled easily. "I'll be going out for a little while, Vi, but I should be back before you're done here."

"Not a problem, Mr. Kayjay," she assured me, having regained her composure. "I'll hold down the fort until I'm finished. You want I should answer the phone?"

"Certainly," I said. "If someone should call, just jot down the message. There's a pad and pen by the phone in the kitchen."

"Righty-ho," she said before moving past me and clumping down the stairs. I shook my head at the sound. Graceful she was not.

I nipped into the bathroom, remembering belatedly that I had never taken my morning pill. I had been so caught up in writing that I had forgotten it until now. Timing isn't all that critical with the medication, as long as I take a pill every twelve hours or so. Being a few hours late was no biggie, but I shouldn't go much longer without one.

The bathroom gleamed with cleanliness, not that it was all that messy before Violet's ministrations, mind you. Still, I was pleased with her work. I opened the cabinet and reached for the pill bottle. Twisting off the cap, I tilted the bottle and shook a pill out into my hand. I popped the pill into my mouth and swallowed it dry, then replaced the cap and restored the bottle to its place on the shelf.

In my bedroom I stripped off the slightly disreputable shirt and jogging pants I wear when I write and replaced them with a suit and tie. When I appear in the village, I like to look my best. Besides, I need to keep as much skin covered as possible. The medication helps with the sunlight, but the less flesh I expose to the sun's rays, the better I feel.

Collecting hat, gloves, and sunglasses from the table downstairs near the front door, I called to Violet to let her know I was leaving, then let myself out.

The day was cool and cloudy, a perfect late October day. The village was resplendent in its autumn finery, the trees sporting lovely red and gold. A brisk walk down the lane took me past St. Ethelwold's Church to what passed for the village High Street, and I paused at the window of the bookshop, The Book Chase, to examine the display.

I groaned in annoyance. I might have known that the presence of Zeke Harwood in Snupperton Mumsley would bring out the proprietor's mercenary instincts. Stacks of Harwood's latest volume of decorating tips crowded the window, and a sign advertised that Zeke Harwood would be signing the book that evening at seven. Trevor Chase, the owner of the shop, had to sell books in order to stay in business, but I deplored the fact that he had to cater to the public in such an obvious way. No doubt the shop would be mobbed.

I turned away from The Book Chase, my desire to browse the shelves fading away. Instead, I might as well toddle along to the pub and see what might be going on there.

Snupperton Mumsley's one pub, the rather prosaically named Hare and Hound, dated from the sixteenth century. What might have been charming, had any of the Elizabethan origins been left untouched, or at least updated with care, was instead modernized into bland and utilitarian. Despite the fact that it lacked any distinction in appearance, it did have a good reputation for its food and drink, and I knew that if Giles were truly lunching somewhere in the village with Cliff Weatherstone, I'd find them here.

Not, of course, that I was specifically looking for them. But I couldn't deny a certain curiosity, and as long as I was at loose ends, I might as well see what was going on.

I paused just inside the door of the pub and removed my hat, gloves, and sunglasses. The lunch crowd had settled in, and there were few seats available. I sauntered up to the bar and ordered a half of mine host's best dark ale. After paying for it, I picked up the glass and took a sip. I had never developed a liking for ale when I was alive, and being dead hadn't changed my taste all that much. I couldn't stand around in the pub drinkless without attracting notice, however, so I usually held on to a glass until I could discreetly tip the contents into one of the sad-looking plants the pub sported as decoration.

I moved to the end of the bar so that I could see around to the back of the pub where there were several tables, each ensconced in its own little nook with walls that reached nearly to the ceiling. There, in the farthest corner, huddled Giles and Cliff Weatherstone, chatting over their pints and gazing soulfully, no doubt, into each other's eyes.

Giles had his back to me, and Weatherstone seemed so intent upon Giles that I doubted he would notice if I moved closer. The table in the alcove next to theirs was vacant, luckily for me, and I made my way to it quickly and quietly. Neither of them paid any attention as I sidled near them, my face averted, and sat down with my back to the wall between my table and theirs. Since I hadn't ordered anything to eat at the bar, perhaps my luck would hold, and the barmaid would leave me alone long enough for me to hear what was going on at the next table.

"So why do you keep working for him if he doesn't appreciate you?" Cliff Weatherstone asked.

Giles laughed. "He appreciates my work, Cliff. That's not the problem."

"I get you," Cliff said, sniggering in response. "It's all professional, and you wish it were more personal. Naughty, Giles, very naughty. It's not a good idea to mix business with pleasure."

"There doesn't seem to be much danger of that with Simon," Giles said, his tone sour.

I itched to pour the contents of my glass over his head. The ungrateful wretch!

"I swear he's got a heart of stone," Giles said, "or else he's got absolutely no interest in sex."

"If he's managed to keep his hands off you this long," Cliff said, "he must be dead."

Very funny, Cliff, I thought. *Little do you know.*

"He's different, no doubt about that," Giles said, sighing. "But enough about Simon. Tell me more about your work. It sounds quite glamorous."

"Yeah, right," Cliff snorted. "Glamorous, sure. Most of the time it's bloody hard work. And I don't mind telling you putting up with that berk is enough to drive anyone round the bend. You have no idea what he's like."

"I think I'm beginning to have an idea," Giles said. "But he seems quite fond of you."

"Don't believe everything you see," Cliff said. His voice had turned ugly.

"Sounds like he's done something pretty nasty to you, then," Giles said.

Cliff snorted. "He's damn lucky I haven't slipped poison into his tea, I can tell you that!"

Chapter Four

Q*uelle surprise,* I thought. So Zeke Harwood's minions
hated him. Big whoop.

"Heavens, Cliff," Giles protested mildly. "Whatever has
the man done to you?"

There was a pause, while Cliff took a long draught of
whatever he was drinking. I thought for a moment he might
shrug off Giles's question, but then he answered. "The
bloody bastard has stuck a knife in my back, that's what!"

"What do you mean?" Giles asked.

"He's going off to the States, isn't he, to build on the success of "Très Zeke" and that one appearance on "Oprah,"
and guess who's not being asked to go along? The ungrateful sod is dumping me, after we've worked together so
closely for the past three years. He finally decided to tell
me this morning." He made a sound of disgust into his
drink. "Never mind how hard I've had to work to make
him look good and sound good and get the right guests for
the show."

"When is all this going to take place?"

"The program we're going to do here," Cliff said, "is
the last time I'll work with His Majesty. Then he's resting

for two weeks while he gets ready for the States. When he and his little crew board the plane at Heathrow, Yours Truly will be left behind."

"That's too bad, Cliff," Giles said in a comforting tone, "but surely someone as talented as you won't have to look around very long for another job. Everyone will know how successful you've been with Harwood."

"Oh, probably," Cliff said, a bit too casually. "But I was looking forward to getting a toe in the door, so to speak, in the States. This could have been my chance to make some connections there."

"I'm sure you'll get your chance," Giles said. "Besides, if Harwood is a big flop in the States, you wouldn't want to be a part of that."

Cliff laughed heartily. "The sod isn't going to flop, Giles. You know how the Yanks eat up anything with an English accent, even Zeke bloody Harwood. They'll lap up the tripe he ladles out, just you wait and see. He'll be as big as anything on daytime telly there in three months."

"Maybe," Giles said, "but surely even Americans draw the line somewhere."

Cliff laughed again. "Have you seen any of their daytime programs? There is nothing too stupid, nothing too salacious, nothing too degrading for daytime television in the States. They'll eat up our Zeke's decorating advice with a spoon."

"Is he really that good?" Giles asked. "From what little I've seen, some of his work is bloody awful."

Cliff snorted. "In the beginning, he *was* good. Before he got famous. These days, all he believes in is all the lovely lolly he sees rolling in. It doesn't matter much what he does, the ratings keep going up. In fact, the more hideous his work, the more the public seems to love it. And if that cable deal comes through in the States, he'll get even bigger and more outrageous. He'll make millions."

"Nice work if you can get it," Giles said, a touch of envy in his voice.

"Enough of His Majesty," Cliff said. "I'm bloody sick of him. Let's talk about something much more interesting. You."

I rolled my eyes at that one. *How obvious can you get?* I thought. Surely Giles wasn't going to fall for that inane patter, no matter how handsome Cliff was?

I listened for a few minutes longer, but I found I had no stomach for Cliff's nauseating form of seduction. If this was what Giles wanted, then he was welcome to it. I slipped out of my alcove and kept my back to them as I walked away, as quietly and unobtrusively as I could.

Rain clouds had gathered in the sky, making the day considerably darker, so much so that I was able to forego my sunglasses. My mood had darkened along with the sky, and I stumped homeward in no pleasant frame of mind. A pestilence upon Zeke Harwood and his entourage.

"There you are, Mr. Kayjay." Violet's voice sang out as I shut the front door of Laurel Cottage behind me and began divesting myself of hat and sunglasses. "Ooh," she said as she came into the hall to stand and watch me, "don't you look scrumptious in that suit. I do thinks a man looks better in a suit any day, Mr. Kayjay."

"Thank you, Vi," I said, attempting to make my tone as repressive as possible. The last thing I needed was an amorous charwoman. If she kept up this behavior, she would have to find herself another job.

She sensed my reserve, for I could feel her disappointment and hurt. Perhaps she only meant to be friendly, trying to ingratiate herself with a new employer, but I thought it best to nip any incipient crush in the bud. I didn't want her becoming too familiar this early in our relationship as employer and employee.

"From what I can see so far, Vi," I said, deciding to relent a bit, "you're doing a bang-up job with the cleaning. I'm very pleased. Laurel Cottage has never looked so clean and bright."

She preened at that. "Ta, Mr. Kayjay. I do pride meself on me work."

"Quite." I glanced at my watch. "Are you done for the day?"

Violet nodded. "I was just about to go, Mr. Kayjay. No phone messages or anything. So, if that's all, I'll see you on Friday?"

"That's fine, Vi. See you then."

She vanished for a moment, then came back with her purse and sweater in hand. "Ta," she said, as I opened the door for her.

After closing the door behind her, I went upstairs to change clothes. I might as well work for a while this afternoon. I hadn't yet decided whether I would attend Zeke Harwood's signing at The Book Chase this evening. I had no intention of buying one of his books, but I was quite curious to see what kind of crowd he would draw.

Most of the time, when I sat down to write, I had little trouble getting on with the task at hand. This afternoon, however, I found myself feeling restless and less able to concentrate. What was bothering me?

Perhaps what I had heard during my eavesdropping at the pub had unsettled me more than I thought it had. I was very fond of Giles, and I enjoyed our professional relationship. Giles was an exceptionally competent assistant, and certain aspects of my working existence had improved greatly since he had come to work for me.

Giles made it very clear on a regular basis, though, that he hoped for more than a professional relationship with me. I found him very attractive, and I had admitted to myself that he could be more to me than just an assistant. I had continued to hold him at arm's length, however, because I couldn't envision a closer relationship with him without making him acquainted with the truth about what I really was. Therein lay the rub.

How would Giles react if he learned he was attracted to a dead man? I had once gone through the same thing, with my mentor Tristan Lovelace, the handsome and charming vampire who had introduced me to life after death. I had already fallen in love with Tris when he told me the truth about himself, and being devastated by the death of a dear friend from AIDS, I saw existence as a vampire as a way to put myself beyond such a hideous disease.

Giles, though, might react completely differently, and I would find my comfortable existence in Snupperton Mumsley at an end. The thought of giving up this cottage, which was now very much my home, depressed me.

Crikey, but I was getting maudlin! What on earth was the matter with me?

By making a concerted effort, I shut everything else out and began writing. Immersing myself in the troubles of my characters was an excellent panacea.

I worked steadily for several hours, and around five-thirty I switched off the computer and sat back with a feeling of contentment. I had Marianna and Charles right where they belonged, in each other's arms. The end. Time now to relax for a bit, then get ready to face the big event at The Book Chase.

A few minutes before seven, nattily attired once again, I made my way from Laurel Cottage through the cool evening, down the High Street toward the bookstore. Just past St. Ethelwold's Church, where the business area of the High Street began, I stopped in my tracks. Ahead of me, snaking back about two hundred feet from the front door of The Book Chase, was a queue of people. As I watched, more people arrived to add to the growing, chattering group.

I knew Zeke Harwood was insanely popular, but I hadn't

expected to see this many people, in Snupperton Mumsley of all places, turn up for a book signing. Momentarily depressed, I doubted they would show up like this for a signing by Daphne Deepwood or Dorinda Darlington, my two fictional alter egos, much less for the historian Simon Kirby-Jones.

What to do? I considered. I wasn't about to get meekly in the back of the queue and wait my turn to get inside the bookstore, just to observe the gloating author surveying the rapidly vanishing pile of his book, *Très Zeke: Country Living with Style,* being grabbed up by adoring fans. Then I remembered there was another way into the bookstore.

Retracing my route a few paces, I ducked around the corner of the first shop in the block—a pretentious antique "shoppe," which had opened a few months ago—into the lane that ran behind the shops on this side of the High Street. This way I could gain access to the bookstore from the rear. Trevor Chase, the owner, would have hired a caterer to serve food and drinks during the event, and the catering staff would no doubt be using the rear entrance.

As indeed they were. I came through the back door into Trevor's office as a harassed-looking older man with a sweaty brow pushed a tray of champagne-filled glasses in the hands of a younger man in black pants, white shirt, and black bow tie.

"What do you think you're doing?" The older man confronted me as the younger one disappeared through the door leading into the front of the bookstore.

"Don't mind me," I said, smiling. "I'm a good friend of Trevor's, and I've come along to see if I can help out."

He didn't look any too happy at my response. "Long as you stay out of my way, mate."

"Not a problem," I assured him. I advanced to the doorway and pushed the door open, pausing a moment to survey what was going on in the front of the bookstore.

Seated at a table near the front desk, Zeke Harwood gazed with regal composure upon the line of eager fans waiting to have their moment with the famous television personality. Piers Limpley stood beside him, acting as traffic cop, motioning with an impatient wiggle of the fingers for the next in line to approach as the previous supplicant was directed toward the till by one of Trevor's assistants. Two more of Trevor's assistants ran the till and bagged up the books, while Trevor floated around the room, chatting here and there with those who were waiting, with remarkable patience, for their moment to approach Himself.

As far as I could tell, no one needed any assistance from me, which suited me just fine. I preferred to lurk in the background. I found a spot behind one of the bookshelves, out of the main line of traffic, after one of the catering staff muttered "Move your buns, love, or I'll run 'em over" while trying to edge past me with a tray full of empty champagne glasses.

I hoped Trevor wasn't footing the bill for all the drinks and food the crowd was wolfing down, but perhaps Harwood's publisher was paying for it. They sometimes will, for an author who sold as well as Harwood.

Across from me, behind a waist-high range of bookshelves, and not far from where Harwood was signing, Cliff Weatherstone occasionally gave directions to a cameraman who was filming the proceedings. At one point, Cliff glanced over at me, gave a start of recognition, and offered a slight scowl. I beamed back at him, offering him a smile with the highest wattage I could produce, and he blinked and swallowed. He stared at me a moment, then his cameraman elbowed him in the side to get his attention, and he turned away.

I scanned the crowd. Giles was not present, nor was Lady Prunella. I couldn't imagine her attending such an event. It would be too far beneath her dignity. I was rather surprised, given how chummy Giles had become with Cliff Weatherstone, that he wasn't on hand to see how his new friend went about his job. No doubt Cliff would give Giles the details later during an intimate tête-à-tête at Blitherington Hall.

Here and there I spotted persons whom I recognized as locals, but most of the faces were strange. I supposed that Harwood's fans had come from miles around to see him. The village hadn't been this busy in years.

Thanks to the ill-tempered direction of Piers Limpley, the crowd moved through at a brisk pace. He didn't allow anyone to linger more than about forty-five seconds before summoning the next person in line. Throughout it all, Harwood kept a frozen smile on his face, saying very little except "thanks ever so much, dear." Most of those in line were women, but the occasional man twittered just as much as the women were doing.

After about an hour, the crowd began to thin a bit. Giles squeezed in the door and paused to look around. He couldn't bear to wait until later to check up on Cliff, after all. As I watched, he caught Cliff's eye and waved, but to my surprise, he headed toward me through the line of those still waiting.

"Good evening, Simon," he said, coming to a halt beside me. "Somehow I thought you might be here, despite your lack of admiration for the author."

"Do keep your voice down, Giles," I hissed in mock-anger. "If some of these people hear you and take you seriously, they might drag me out of here and tar and feather me."

He laughed. "Ever the drama queen, Simon. I'll protect you, never fear."

"I'm honored, Sir Giles."

His eyes narrowed. "Someone is rather snarky this evening. What's wrong with you?"

I raised an eyebrow. "Why should anything be wrong with me?"

"Something is," he said, his tone playful. "But I shan't belabor the point."

As I studied his handsome face, I found my attention wandering toward the pulse of the veins in his neck. I had never noticed how tempting they were. I felt a strong urge to bend my lips to his neck and nibble at them. For a moment I was convinced that I could actually see the blood moving through the veins. I closed my eyes for a moment, and the odd sensation went away. I opened my eyes again, and Giles was looking at me oddly.

"Are you ill, Simon?" he asked in genuine concern.

"No, I'm fine," I insisted.

"You had the queerest look on your face just now," he said. "Are you certain you're not coming down with something?"

I shook my head.

A scream of outrage claimed our attention, and we both swiveled in surprise to see what was going on.

Zeke Harwood, his face and hair spattered with bright green paint, was now standing, flailing his arms about and sputtering.

"Stop that man!" Piers Limpley shouted.

Chapter Five

By the time everyone in the bookstore overcame the shock of the assault on Zeke Harwood, the man who had dumped paint on the hapless celebrity had barreled out the door and vanished. A couple of the men standing on line attempted to give chase, but people were moving about so, getting in one another's way, that the attempt was doomed to failure.

Piers Limpley and Trevor Chase were now making vain efforts to wipe the paint away from Harwood's face, but succeeded only in smearing it all over themselves and him.

"Good grief," Giles exclaimed. "Why ever would someone want to do such a thing?"

I shrugged, watching the proceedings with great amusement. "Too bad, that shade of green is simply *not* his color. I'd have gone for dark red myself."

"Simon!" Giles protested, then couldn't help himself. He burst out laughing.

Heads swiveled in our direction, and we became the cynosure of many pairs of accusing eyes. Their beloved decorating guru had been most grievously attacked, and here we were, making a joke of it.

Which was, no doubt, the point of it all. Zeke Harwood had not been seriously injured, I fancied, unless you counted the dent in his dignity. Cliff Weatherstone, I was quick to note, had kept his cameraman filming everything. If they had got a clear shot of the man who had thrown the paint, the police might soon track the culprit down.

Piers Limpley led the dripping celebrity from the room, toward the back where the bookstore's loo was located, while Trevor claimed the attention of those milling about, clutching unsigned books.

"In view of what has just occurred," Trevor said, his mellow voice roughened by frustration, "I'm sure you will all understand that Mr. Harwood will be unable to continue with the event this evening. We will make every effort, however, to ensure that any of you who still wish to have signed copies of his book will have them. Please see me or one of my staff before you leave. Thank you all for attending, and, again, my apologies for what has happened this evening."

A buzz of grumbling arose, and I didn't envy Trevor and his staff having to deal with the disappointed Harwood fans. Cliff Weatherstone and his cameraman were packing up equipment as I strode over to ask Cliff a few questions. Giles trailed along behind me.

"Evening, Weatherstone," I said. I nodded at the cameraman who, intent on taking care of his equipment, paid no attention to us.

"Good evening, Kirby-Jones," Cliff said, his voice gruff. "Giles. Didn't expect to see you here."

"I decided at the last minute to pop along," Giles said, offering a sunny smile, to which Cliff responded immediately with a broad smile of his own.

"Quite a surprising turn of events, don't you think, Weatherstone?" I claimed his attention. "Has anything like this ever happened to Harwood before?"

"No," Cliff said, shaking his head in puzzlement. "And I can't think why it should happen now, of all times."

"Oh, you can't?" I had my own ideas about that. If Cliff were as angry with Harwood as he claimed to be earlier, when lunching with Giles at the pub, I wouldn't put it past him to have arranged this little incident. He might be trying to appear regretful, but I could feel strong waves of amusement and self-satisfaction emanating from him. "But I'm sure you got the whole thing on tape, so the police won't have any trouble tracking down the person who assaulted Harwood."

The cameraman cut me a look, then busied himself stowing away the rest of his gear. Cliff cleared his throat uncomfortably. "I'm afraid we missed that bit," he said, his face reddening under my disbelieving scrutiny.

"Oh, really," I said, turning to Giles. "They missed that bit, did you hear?"

"Yes, Simon, my ears are still in perfect working order," Giles responded with some asperity.

"Quite a lucky break for Mr. Paint Man, don't you think?" I said, not bothering to hide the sarcasm.

"Just what are you getting at, Kirby-Jones?" Cliff demanded. Again, the cameraman caught my eyes with his, then looked quickly away. He knew something, but I wouldn't get it out of him with Cliff standing over him. Something to follow up later, if I had the opportunity.

"Nothing," I said airily. "Just remarking upon an interesting coincidence."

"Simon," Giles said, catching at my arm. "Behave yourself, and stop acting as if Cliff were the one who threw paint on the man."

"Heaven forfend, Giles," I replied, throwing my hands up as if to ward off an attack.

"Really, Simon," Giles said, "sometimes you are the limit. You truly are."

As he stood there, face flushed in annoyance, I once again became aware of the pulse beating so strongly in his neck. I took a step toward him. All I could think about in that moment was placing my lips on that lovely vein of his, feeling the throbbing of the blood against my mouth.

"Simon!"

The sharp tone of Giles's voice recalled me to my senses. I shook my head as if to clear it. What on earth was the matter with me?

"You've gone all over queer, Simon. Are you certain that you're not ill?" Giles watched me with concern and not a little alarm, his irritation supplanted.

"My dear boy, I've been all over queer since I was fifteen," I told him, attempting to make a joke of it.

Giles rolled his eyes, while behind me I could hear the cameraman sniggering.

"Really, Simon," Giles said, a smile tugging at the corners of his mouth.

"I'm fine," I assured him. I turned back to Cliff Weatherstone. "Is Piers Limpley reporting this to the police, do you think?"

Weatherstone shook his head. "No, I shouldn't think so. This isn't exactly the kind of publicity that our Zeke cares for. He'd look a right prat, wouldn't he, if this made it onto the telly." He couldn't suppress a grin at the thought of that.

"Then you'd better hope that the footage you shot doesn't get out of your hands, and into the hands of someone who wouldn't hesitate to use it to embarrass the man." I paused. "But perhaps you didn't get any shots of him with green paint all over him, since you missed getting the man who assaulted him."

Weatherstone glared at me, while the cameraman straightened up. He opened his mouth and began talking, but his accent was one of those nearly impenetrable ones from the north of England that I have yet to master. The gist of what he had to say was, I gathered, that while he hadn't caught the miscreant on tape, he did have some footage of Harwood in the green, as it were.

"Then you'd better guard that tape," I advised him. He winked back at me.

"If you're quite done telling us how to do our jobs, Kirby-Jones," Weatherstone said, icicles dripping from every syllable, "I think we'd better get back to Blitherington Hall. We have more prep work to do for tomorrow's filming." Jerking his head to indicate that the cameraman should follow him, he stalked out of the bookstore.

"Why do you dislike him so, Simon?" Giles asked, a curious expression on his face.

"He's far too slick for my tastes, dear boy," I said airily. "And I'm convinced he knows more about the little brouhaha tonight than he's letting on."

"First of all, Simon, I'm not your *dear boy*, as you've made abundantly clear on any number of occasions, so stop patronizing me." Giles fairly spit the words at me. I had never seen him so angry. "Second, I happen to think Cliff is rather a nice bloke, and devilishly attractive. You're being petty and offensive, and you know it."

To say I was taken aback at the vehemence of Giles's defense of his new inamorato would be an understatement. Giles's infatuation with the man must be more serious than I had guessed. Surely he wasn't that shallow, to fall for a pretty face and a swaggering manner? Perhaps I had misjudged him after all.

"Sorry, I'm sure, Giles," I said, in a tone far milder than I thought I could manage. "I do beg your pardon."

"As well you ought," Giles said, still huffy with me. "In view of everything that is planned for tomorrow at Blitherington Hall, I'm afraid I must ask you for another day's leave. I had better be on hand to keep an eye on everything."

I hoped I hadn't annoyed him so much that he wanted

to quit his job with me. Time to offer an olive branch, it seemed. "Certainly, Giles. I had been going to suggest that myself. Your mother will need you tomorrow, and I had already decided that we both deserved a break from work." I hesitated a moment, for once uncertain of his reaction. "I had even thought I might come along and observe, if you don't think I'd be in the way. I'd love the opportunity to observe how the television crew works. It could come in handy for a book one of these days."

His handsome face had softened at my apology. He reached out and squeezed my arm. "You're always welcome at Blitherington Hall, Simon, you know that. I might need you on hand to keep me from throttling my mother, who's bound to make a complete nuisance of herself." He grinned at the thought.

"I'd be delighted, de . . . , um, Giles," I caught myself in time.

"See you tomorrow morning, then, about ten-ish?"

"Yes, that sounds good," I said. He smiled at me again, genuine warmth in his face this time, then made his way out of the bookstore.

I glanced around. Only a few diehard souls were left, still hanging on to their copies of Harwood's book, vainly hoping he would reappear. Since neither Zeke Harwood nor Piers Limpley had shown themselves in the front of the store again, I assumed that they had made their escape through the back door. Probably they were already back at Blitherington Hall, doing what they could to clean up Harwood in time for tomorrow's filming.

I hung around for a bit longer, waiting to ask Trevor if there were anything I could do to help. When Trevor did appear, he waved away my offer, thanking me, but insisting that he and his staff would take care of everything. "I'm sorry for your sake, Trevor," I said, "that someone made such a mess of things."

Trevor smiled wearily. "Despite it all, we sold quite a lot of books, Simon, so it wasn't a total loss." He leaned closer, and his voice dropped to a whisper. "And just between you and me, I'm not all that sorry someone gave that idiot what he deserved."

"Oh, really?" I asked, inviting further tidbits.

Trevor shook his head. "He was impossible from the beginning. The table and the chair we had set up for him were wrong and had to be replaced. Then we had the wrong kind of pens for him to sign with. There was a draft. One of my staff was wearing a type of cologne he found obtrusive. On and on and on he went, one complaint after another. And he kept reminding me what an enormous favor he was doing me even to set foot in my little shop, because normally he only signs his books in large stores that can accommodate the thousands of fans who usually show up." He gritted his teeth. "He let me know it was my fault that there were only about two hundred people here tonight. Evidently I hadn't done enough to publicize the event to suit His Nibs."

"What a berk," I said in complete sympathy.

"I only wish that the cameraman had recorded it all, so I could steal the tape and sell it to one of the tabloids. A right prat that would make him look." Trevor's face brightened for a moment at the thought of getting back at the obnoxious author.

I laughed. "He may yet get his comeuppance, Trevor, and it might be more than a bit of green paint."

He joined in my laughter as I bade him a good night.

I whistled as I walked back down the High Street toward Laurel Cottage. The evening had turned out to be far more entertaining than I had hoped, and tomorrow held promise as well.

Chapter Six

Half an hour or so after I had taken my morning pill, I felt better. Yesterday had been rather unsettling, for a number of reasons. My little spats with Giles, those odd sensations of wanting to bite his neck, were strange. I had felt quite unlike my usual self. But perhaps I hadn't been rigorous enough about taking my pills at proper intervals. The medication worked best, I had been warned from the beginning, when taken exactly as directed. I couldn't afford a relapse to the old ways.

I shuddered. The thought of sucking blood and hiding away during the day gave me the creeps. I had better get one of those watches with an alarm, to remind me to take my pills.

The writing went more smoothly after the pill kicked in, because I felt better able to concentrate. Then, around nine, my concentration began to wander. With a start, I realized I had been listening for Giles's arrival at the front door.

But of course Giles wasn't coming to work today. Instead he was staying at home, playing Lord of the Manor, keeping an eye on Harwood, Weatherstone, and the film crew. I debated for a moment whether to stay home and work after all, or to give in to my curiosity and go to Blitherington Hall to watch the proceedings.

Curiosity won.

Shortly before ten o'clock, properly attired against the weak morning sun, I drove the Jag the short distance to the Hall. Thompson answered the knock on the front door quickly, almost as if he had been waiting just for me.

"Morning, Thompson," I said, handing him my hat and gloves. "How are you today?"

"Fine, Professor," he said. He persisted in calling me this, though I assured him that plain Mr. Kirby-Jones would do, knowing that he'd stick at calling me Simon. Such informality would never pass muster with Lady Prunella.

"Sir Giles invited me along to watch the filming," I explained, after assuring him that I too was fine. "Is he about somewhere?"

Clutching my hat and gloves, Thompson tottered toward a table to set them down. "You'll find the young master in the library, Professor."

"He's not watching the filming?"

"No, sir," Thompson said with a slight frown. "No one is allowed to watch, per Mr. Harwood's instructions."

"Ah, yes," I said. "I had forgotten. Mr. Harwood does his makeovers in secret, then unveils everything on camera. I don't imagine that Lady Prunella is very keen on being surprised."

Thompson's lips contracted in a prim smile. "As you say, Professor."

I wondered what fireworks I had missed already. "Then I'll be off to the library, Thompson."

"Very good, sir." He toddled off in the direction of the kitchen, and I wandered down the hall toward the library. I knocked on the door, waited a moment, then opened the door and walked in.

"I do beg your pardon," I said, halting abruptly just inside the door. "I had no idea I would be interrupting a private meeting."

Giles sat at his desk, poring over some document. Cliff Weatherstone, looking indecently handsome in tight leather pants and an even tighter-fitting shirt, leaned over Giles, one hand casually—or was it possessively?—resting on Giles's shoulder.

"Good morning, Simon," Giles responded, his attention still focused on the papers on his desk. "Cliff and I were just looking over the contract."

Weatherstone straightened up, his hand still on Giles's shoulder, and smiled at me. "Good morning, Professor."

"Morning, Weatherstone. The country air must agree with you. I trust you're enjoying your stay at Blitherington Hall."

"Oh, my, yes," Weatherstone assured me. "Blitherington Hall has certain amenities I hadn't expected to find. And there's nothing like country air and a little exercise to make one feel quite pleased with life."

Judging by his self-satisfied tone, I had little doubt as to the type of exercise he had enjoyed. And in whose bedroom he had done so.

Giles had been paying no attention to us. He dropped the papers onto his desk and leaned back in his chair. For the first time he appeared to notice the proprietary hand resting on his shoulder. He pushed back his chair and stood up, forcing Cliff Weatherstone to step away from him. Weatherstone frowned.

"I cannot say that I am pleased with this bit about secrecy," Giles said, returning Weatherstone's frown. "How can we be assured that Harwood won't make the room into some kind of travesty, just because he would find it amusing to do so?"

Weatherstone folded his arms, and I watched with interest as the muscles in his arms twitched. He was annoyed, but whether with me or Giles, I could not tell. "It's all a matter of taste, Giles," he said. "I really do not think you have anything to worry about. Zeke can be capricious, but he wouldn't deliberately set out to ruin a room."

"I sincerely trust not," Giles said with some asperity, "or there will be the very devil to pay. Neither I, nor my mother, is anyone to be crossed lightly."

Weatherstone made a mocking bow. "Of course not, Sir Giles."

Giles flushed but wisely chose to say nothing in response to Weatherstone's bitchiness. Instead he turned to me. "I'm delighted to see you this morning, Simon. As it turns out, I might as well have come to work today, because I really can do nothing here. Harwood refuses to allow anyone except his crew into the drawing room, so there's not a thing for any of us to see."

"The day is still young," I said, smiling. "If you'd like, we can return to Laurel Cottage and attend to some things that need both our attention. I'm sure Cliff here has things to do, like supervising the filming, or whatever it is he actually does."

Weatherstone glowered at me, and I smiled sweetly back at him.

There came a discreet knock at the door, and Thompson entered. "I beg your pardon, Sir Giles," he said, "but perhaps you might want to come and have a talk with Lady Prunella and Mr. Harwood. They are presently having a discussion." The slight emphasis he placed upon that last word left little doubt that Giles was needed to intervene between the two.

"Right away, Thompson," Giles said. He rubbed his forehead, as if to assuage some kind of pain, then walked out of the room. Weatherstone and I followed, as Thompson stood aside, holding the door.

Down the hall, Zeke Harwood stood with his back

against the drawing room doors. Lady Prunella walked
back and forth in front of him, her arms waving in the air
as she talked. A small crowd of staff had gathered a few
feet away, and among them I spotted Jessamy Cholmondley-
Pease looming over them in her impossibly high heels.

"What seems to be the matter, Mummy?" Giles asked
as Lady Prunella paused for breath. He came to a halt near
his agitated parent.

Lady Prunella halted in mid-stride. "This . . . this *person* absolutely *refuses* to let me inside my *own* drawing
room. It is unsupportable! To be refused *entrance* to a
room in my own home!"

"As I was endeavoring to remind dear Lady Prudence,"
Harwood purred, "no one, and absolutely no one, except
me and my crew are allowed in the room I'm redecorating
while work is in progress. Even if the queen herself desired
admittance, I would have to deny her, at the risk of being
accused of treasonous behavior." He tittered.

Really, the man was far too full of himself. I could not
deny, however, the pleasure of watching Lady Prunella's
being prevented from doing something. Her face had
turned the most amusing shade of puce.

"There!" Lady Prunella said. "You see what I mean! The
utter *vulgarity* of this person. To take the *queen's* name in
vain in such a *common* manner." She stood glaring at Harwood as if he were the veriest dirt beneath her feet.

It was a wonder the poor woman didn't drop dead from
a stroke, right on the spot.

"Now, Mummy," Giles said, attempting a placatory tone,
"I'm sure Mr. Harwood did not mean to offend you, but
I'm afraid that we have no choice. According to the contract we signed, we have agreed that he and his crew may
work for two days without our being able to see any of
what he's doing. Surely you haven't forgotten? After all,
you watch his television program all the time."

"Exactly, Lady Prudence," Harwood said. "An artist such as I cannot have his vision tainted while he works. We did consult about the work, but beyond that, you must not interfere. It simply is not to be allowed."

"I'll thank you to remember my name," Lady Prunella snapped at him. "It is *not* Lady Prudence, it is Lady Prunella, you half-wit!"

"Whatever," Harwood said airily, his hand flapping in the air.

Lady Prunella stepped forward, her right hand raised as if to strike the supercilious git, but Giles intervened. "Now, Mummy, you mustn't upset yourself so. I've no doubt that you'll be delighted once you see what Mr. Harwood has done with the drawing room. Tomorrow night, Mr. Harwood?"

"Yes, Sir Giles," Harwood said. "We shall unveil the room in all its splendor tomorrow evening. Then you shall eat your words, madam." He sniffed.

Lady Prunella turned to her son. "But, Giles," she wailed, "red!"

Giles was startled. "What do you mean, Mummy? Red?"

"He's going to paint the room *red!*" Lady Prunella's pitch became shriller with each syllable.

"How on earth do you know that?" Harwood asked, frowning.

"I saw the cans of paint," Lady Prunella shouted. "You idiot! I told you that I cannot *abide* red, and yet you are going to paint my walls *red!*"

"Madam," Harwood said, crossing his arms protectively over his chest, "there is little I can do about the absolute lack of good taste exhibited by the majority of the rooms in this monstrous pile of a house you call your home. But I can, and I will, rescue at least one of the rooms. Your drawing room, by the time I have finished with it, will be the one room in this whole bloody mausoleum that has style and personality. If you had any sense whatsoever, you would be grateful that I have deigned to come here and perform an act of the most extreme charity." His eyes narrowed. "Instead, you stand there screaming at me like the commonest fishwife and making yourself absolutely ridiculous."

He paused to take a deep breath. "Furthermore, the fact that I am able to continue under such circumstances is a testament to my commitment to my work and my artistic vision. I will let nothing, not even you, stand in my way."

"You, sir, are the most insulting *worm* it has ever been *my* misfortune to meet." Lady Prunella glared back at him. I had to admire the old girl for her spunk. Almost anyone else would have wilted before the challenge presented by Zeke Harwood. "Stand aside and let me in that room!"

"Over my dead body!" Harwood said, splaying his arms against the doors. I noted, without much surprise, that he was enjoying every moment of this tasteless little drama.

"What a *thoroughly* delightful idea," Lady Prunella said, her face as red as the walls of her drawing room might be. "If you use that red paint, you'll wish you *were* dead!"

Chapter Seven

Zeke Harwood threw back his head and laughed. "Absolutely delicious, Lady Priscilla! Such drama! Such pathos!" He laughed again. "The punters will go mad with joy."

"What?" Lady Prunella stared blankly at her adversary.

Harwood ignored her. "Did you get all that?"

Without our noticing it, a cameraman had been discreetly filming all that had just transpired. He took the portable video camera off his shoulder and nodded at Harwood. "Got it all, guv," he said. At least, that's what I thought he said, though his accent was so thick, I couldn't be completely sure.

"Do you mean to say," Giles had approached Harwood and prodded his chest with one menacing finger, "that this entire little drama was manufactured for the benefit of your program?"

I could sense the rage boiling up inside of Giles, and I could not blame him. To think that Harwood had manipulated Lady Prunella into such an outburst simply to make his program more dramatic was nauseating. I was no great fan of Lady Prunella, but this was too dirty a trick to play, even upon her.

Harwood was unrepentant. "The more drama the better, mate. The viewers expect it, and they'll get a right zing out of seeing Lady Primrose nearly off her rocker at the thought of me painting the room red." He was so tickled with himself that he started giggling. "I knew that red paint would wind her up." He sputtered the words out in between bursts of giggling.

All this time, Lady Prunella had stood with her mouth opening and closing as she tried to form words, but she never managed to utter a syllable. "Don't mind him, Mummy," Giles said, putting an arm around her. "I'll get this sorted out."

"Nothing you can do about it, sport," Harwood assured him airily. "Just take a butcher's at the contract if you doubt me."

Giles forbore to say anything further. Leading his mother gently away, he left Harwood still chortling with self-satisfaction over his cleverness. Cliff Weatherstone, who had been hovering in the background all this time, stepped forward. "I want to talk to you, Zeke, about this. Come on."

"Oh, dear," Harwood said. "Is Cliffie-Wiffie angry with poor Zeke? Just because he's having to do Cliffie's job for him, while Cliffie pants around after his latest boytoy like a bitch in heat?"

Someone who sounded suspiciously like Jessamy Cholmondley-Pease tittered in the background, and I took note once more of the crowd that had been assembled for some time, watching the scenes play out. They were getting quite a show.

Weatherstone's face darkened, and he raised his left arm as if to strike Harwood. Harwood didn't flinch, as if dar-

ing the younger man to hit him. "You are the absolute
bloody limit, Zeke," Weatherstone said. His teeth were
clenched so tight, I could hardly understand what he was
saying.

"Just don't forget who the star is here," Harwood said.
If he had used that tone with me, I would have removed a
certain bit of his anatomy—permanently. Weatherstone
didn't appear to be man enough, however. Such a surprise.

While Weatherstone stood glowering in impotence,
Harwood turned and opened the doors to the drawing
room. Before any of us could catch a glimpse of what was
going on inside, he had slammed the doors shut again.

Humiliated, Weatherstone slunk away, the handy cameraman trailing behind him. The rest of the assembled company,
mostly the villagers who had been hired on as temporary
help, drifted back to whatever they had been doing beforehand. Jessamy Cholmondley-Pease remained where she
was, trying her best to look as if she belonged there.

I stood for a moment, debating what I should do. Go
seek out Giles and Lady Prunella and attempt to help
smooth ruffled feathers? Or was there something else I
could do?

Recalling that the drawing room had another entrance,
from the terrace outside, I left through the front door and
walked quickly around to the side of Blitherington Hall.
Sure enough, Harwood and his crew were using the side
entrance, rather large and gaudy French windows, as their
main point of access to the drawing room.

I stepped over a mass of cables and into the room. A
minion, short and terribly self-important, accosted me in a
light baritone to inform me that members of the family
were not allowed to watch, according to the contract.

"I am not a member of the family, and I have not signed
any kind of contract. Do be a good creature, and step
aside. I shan't get in anyone's way, I assure you."

The minion, clad in a T-shirt emblazoned with the "Très Zeke" logo, scowled and muttered something like, "We'll see about that." Turning on its heel, it stomped away. I think it was female, judging from the shape of its denim-clad posterior, but the rest of it was so sexless, who could tell?

I had a moment or two to glance around before Minion Number One returned with Minions Two and Three, who were considerably larger and most definitely masculine. "Sorry, sir, but you'll have to go. No one but the crew is allowed in here while we're working." This came from Minion Two, as I dubbed him.

When I stood there without saying a word or offering to move, Minion Three exhibited a marked lack of patience and laid a rough hand on my arm. Casually I shook it off. "I don't think so," I said in a pleasant tone. "I wouldn't advise attempting to move me without my permission."

Three, who was several inches taller and quite a few pounds heavier than I, apparently didn't believe me, because he placed his hand on my arm again. I don't think I actually broke any of his fingers when I removed said hand, but he squealed just as loudly as if I had. He had no idea, naturally, how strong I am. That is one thing my magic little pills haven't affected. I am much stronger than most live men, and while I can't pick up an automobile or leap tall buildings in a single bound, I don't have to worry about physical threats from buffed-up interior decorating queens like Minions Two and Three.

"You might want to put some ice on that," I advised unlucky Three as he continued to whimper. "Do run along now, before the swelling gets any worse."

All three of them backed off at that point, apparently having decided they had rather face the wrath of Harwood than deal with me. I grinned. I do relish these little Clint Eastwood moments, as infrequent as they are.

No one else in the room had paid much attention to the foregoing mini-drama. Harwood was deeply engrossed in a conversation with his sister, Dittany, and his housekeeper, Mrs. Rhys-Morgan. They both wore paint-daubed smocks, and I could see that they had been at work in the room, painting the walls a pleasing shade of pale blue. Not red, I was relieved to see, though I noticed a can of it on the floor with the other cans. The red paint really had been nothing more than a decoy, as it were, to get Lady Prunella riled up. Harwood was quite a piece of work.

Piers Limpley labored in another corner of the room, sorting through fabric samples with yet another worker in a "Très Zeke" shirt.

There were drop cloths everywhere, and most of the furniture had been moved out of the room, along with the carpets. The room seemed to be in the midst of a makeover, which is exactly what Harwood was supposed to be giving it. Members of the crew filming the work were involved in various tasks, adjusting lighting and so on.

I had satisfied myself on the main point that had prompted me to defy Harwood's mandate that no one witness the work-in-progress. He really did seem to be doing a legitimate redo of the room and not preparing some elaborate practical joke at Lady Prunella's expense, just for the sake of his program. Surely he had had his fun and would now concentrate on the real job.

Now, on to my second reason for having bearded the lion in his den. I cleared my throat, and Piers Limpley glanced my way. Thrusting the fabric samples into the hands of an assistant, he strode over to me.

"Professor Kirby-Jones, isn't it?" His tone was cordial, but he barely masked his irritation.

I nodded. "Good morning, Mr. Limpley. It seems as if all is going well here."

"Yes, it is, Professor," he said, "but I really must insist that you go. Zeke is adamant about not having anyone outside the crew see the work-in-progress."

"I do understand that, Mr. Limpley," I said, standing my ground. He had taken my arm and made an ineffective effort to lead me back toward the French windows.

"I'm afraid there's something I must discuss with you before I will leave the room."

Exasperated, he dropped his hand from my arm. "And what is that, Professor?"

Without mincing words, I explained the nasty trick Harwood had played upon Lady Prunella. "I cannot believe that Harwood is seriously considering using that footage for his program," I said in conclusion. "It makes him look completely ridiculous and incredibly unpleasant."

Limpley refused to meet my eyes. "Zeke has a fine sense of what is appropriate for his program and what his viewers will enjoy. I'm sure Lady Prunella will come to find the whole episode quite amusing when she has had more time to reflect upon it."

"You don't really believe that, do you?"

"What I believe is of no import whatsoever, Professor," he said, his voice devoid of inflection. "What matters is what Zeke thinks and wants, and if Zeke wants to use this for the program, then it will be used. Case closed."

"That is really most unfortunate," I said.

"And what little plots are we hatching here with the handsome professor?" Zeke Harwood had caught sight of me in conference with his right-hand man and had come to find out what was going on. He fluttered his eyelashes at me, attempting a flirtatious gesture, but I could tell his heart wasn't in it. He just did it because it was expected of him.

"I was simply explaining to Mr. Limpley that I thought

it would be rather unfortunate for all concerned if you used that nasty little trick you played upon Lady Prunella on your program."

Harwood frowned at the coldness of my tone, but before he could respond, both his sister Dittany and his house-keeper, Mrs. Rhys-Morgan, had joined us. "What is it, Zeke? What's going on?" Mrs. Rhys-Morgan demanded in her husky voice.

"What have you done now, Zeke?" Dittany asked with considerably more perspicacity.

Before Harwood could respond, I told them.

"Oh, really, Zeke," Dittany said in disgust. "That poor woman. She didn't deserve such a nasty trick. How could you?"

"Really, Zeke," Mrs. Rhys-Morgan said, chiming right in. "Most unsporting of you, I must say."

Harwood's face turned mulish. "I don't care what you say, any of you. The cow had it coming to her, and my viewers will eat it up. You wait and see. This will be the highest-rated episode of 'Très Zeke' yet."

"Your ratings are high enough, Zeke," Dittany protested, "without you resorting to something like that. I really think you should reconsider. It's going to make you look rather mean, don't you think?"

"Yes, Zeke," Mrs. Rhys-Morgan said. "You don't want to look mean, now do you?" She beamed at him. "Everyone admires your style and flair, and the witty way in which you present each program. You wouldn't want your sense of humor getting you into trouble, now would you?"

The playful tone had evidently struck the wrong note with Harwood. He dug in his heels. "I don't care what any of you think, I'm going to do exactly as I please. I think you all need to remember just who is in charge here, after all."

"You don't ever let us bloody forget it," Dittany said,

her voice so full of bitterness even her brother was taken aback.

He eyed her with loathing. "Then if it bothers you that much, you can go find another job somewhere, now can't you? I don't need you. If you weren't family, you'd have been out on the street long before now."

"You bloody bastard!" Dittany said. "You had better watch your mouth, or you'll regret it. I *am* family, and you had better remember exactly what that means." She turned and stalked off.

Harwood uttered a word, in a rather loud voice, which is often vulgarly used to refer to a certain part of the female anatomy.

Dittany halted in her tracks, turned slowly, then came back to where we stood. "It would be such a pleasure," she said, enunciating each word slowly in order to inject the maximum amount of venom, "to see you in hell where you belong." Then she slapped him so hard, he staggered backward and almost tripped over a can of paint.

Chapter Eight

What a loving family the Harwoods were, I mused as I watched Zeke Harwood flailing his arms about to keep from falling. He finally managed to right himself, and his face had flushed a deep red with the effort. He stood with his legs astride the can of paint that had almost tripped him, his sides heaving from the exertion of staying upright.

Dittany had paid not the slightest attention to him after the slap. Instead she had, with great calm, gone back to work, her back to all of us. I thought that was rather a dangerous position in the circumstances, because Zeke Harwood seemed like the vindictive type to me. I wouldn't have put it past him to throw something at her to knock her over.

Moira Rhys-Morgan must have been of the same mind, for she moved to stand in front of Harwood, blocking his view of his sister. "Zeke, dear," she said, her tone low and soothing, "perhaps you'd like to come upstairs with me for a little while and put your feet up? Or perhaps a nice walk in the garden? There's a love. Do come along."

She continued to talk to him, her voice never varying

from its honeyed sounds. Whether it was her attentions
that did the trick, or whether his sister's threat had some
deeper meaning, he decided to retire from the field of battle. Yielding to Mrs. Rhys-Morgan, he let her lead him out
the French windows.

I had stepped a few feet to one side during this delicious
little fracas, and Piers Limpley seemed to have forgotten
my presence. He walked over to Dittany Harwood and
put an arm around her shoulders. He whispered to her, but
with my sensitive ears, I could make out every word.

"Dittany, my dear, was that wise? You know what he's
like. He'll find some way to make you pay for that. You really shouldn't have done that."

Dittany shrugged off his arm. "Oh, Piers, don't be such
an old woman. Zeke may well try to get back at me, but if
he's not careful, he's going to find a few little choice family
secrets on the front page of the most scandalous rag I can
find. I am utterly weary of putting up with him and his
ridiculous behavior."

"You can't mean that!" Piers hissed in her ear. "Think
what it would mean for all of us. Our jobs! What would
we all do?"

"Oh, go away, Piers, you're making me excessively
tired," Dittany said. She refused to pay any further attention to him and instead focused on the job at hand, painting carefully around the edges of the fireplace.

I had seen more than enough. I made my way back
through the room toward the French windows. Minion
Three, who evidently was just returning from having
soaked his fingers in cold water, gave me a nasty look as I
met him at the door. But he did step aside and let me pass.

"Too kind," I murmured.

I had better keep an eye out for him. There's nothing
like a vindictive queen with a grudge. I should know.

Once back inside the front hall, I decided to seek out

Giles. By now he had surely managed to calm his mother enough, and he might be ready to return with me to Laurel Cottage for the peace and quiet of work.

I tried the library first, and my luck was in. Giles sat at his desk, staring morosely off into space.

"Well, Giles," I said in my cheeriest tone, "are you ready for a spot of work?"

"Oh, Simon," he groaned, "what am I going to do with this unholy mess? Mother has succumbed to a fit of the vapors, something she hasn't done since my father died, and that insufferable idiot is doing heaven knows what in the drawing room."

"No need to worry about the latter, dear boy," I said. "I've just come from the drawing room, and it all actually looks rather good. At least, what they've done so far. Not a jot of red paint in sight."

Giles brightened. "That's something. Now if only I can persuade Harwood not to use that footage of Mummy screaming like a fishwife." His voice trailed off when he caught sight of my face. "He's going to use it, isn't he?"

"Most likely," I said. I gave him a summary of the nasty little scene I had witnessed, and he grimaced. "No doubt that has made him all the more determined to have his way."

"Then curse the day that Mummy ever watched that man's program. What am I going to do, Simon?" He groaned once again. "Mummy expects me to take care of the situation."

This was certainly an interesting turn of events. Once upon a time, Lady Prunella had been wont to take charge of everything, leaving Giles playing second fiddle. But recently, seeing the signs of her son's growing maturity, the dear lady had been loosing the reins a bit and allowing him to handle matters in his own way. Graduation day had come with a vengeance.

"I'm not sure there is much you can do, Giles," I said

bluntly. "Short of bribing the cameraman to lose the videotape."

"Not a bad idea, Simon," Giles said, his face clearing. "But it might be better if I talked to Cliff about it. Perhaps he can persuade the cameraman for me."

"No doubt Cliffie would be delighted to do something for you," I said, my tone waspish despite my best efforts. "Just say 'leap, frog,' and I'm sure he'll ask 'how high?' "

"What on earth does that mean?" Giles asked.

I shook my head in irritation. "A Southernism, Giles. Perfectly clear to anyone where I come from. Pay it no mind." I turned to go. "I shall return to Laurel Cottage to work. I gather you will be too busy here, after all, to get away."

"Don't run off in such a snit, Simon," Giles said tiredly. "You can believe it when I tell you I had much rather go with you to Laurel Cottage than remain in this madhouse." He stood up. "But discretion being the better part of valor and all that, I should remain here to keep an eye on things. If I don't, Mummy's likely to murder someone. Not that I could blame her."

"Good day, Giles," I said. "Perhaps I shall see you tomorrow?"

Giles ignored my childishly spiteful tone. Instead he smiled. "Perhaps you would like to come to dinner tonight? Help me keep an eye on the assorted loonies? I could certainly use your help, Simon."

Touched, and feeling more than a bit ashamed of my little fit of pique, I said, "Of course, dear boy. I should be delighted to render whatever assistance I can. What time?"

"Eight o'clock, rather than the usual seven," Giles said. "These television people keep somewhat later hours than we country bumpkins."

"See you then," I said.

The hallway was empty as I let myself out the front

door of Blitherington Hall. The sky had become overcast, with clouds gathering and portending of rain. Just the kind of day I like.

I drove my car back through the village and parked it at Laurel Cottage, but rather than going inside and getting back to work, I walked down the lane toward the center of the village. I thought I might drop in on Trevor Chase at the bookshop. Perhaps by now Trevor knew something more about the mysterious man who had assaulted Zeke Harwood during the author event at the shop.

The Book Chase was quiet as I entered—not a customer in sight. I called out a greeting, and moments later Trevor emerged from his office in the rear of the shop. "Hullo, Simon," he said, his face brightening. "How are you?"

"Just fine, Trevor, and yourself?"

"Quite well, Simon." He came and perched himself on a stool behind the counter. "Rather glad, actually, for a bit of peace and quiet today."

"Yes, it was a bit tiring, I'm sure, having that big event here."

Trevor nodded. "Events like that are quite helpful for the old bottom line, but they are also incredibly stressful." He sighed. "And to have such an incident occur during the event. Well, you can imagine how distressing that was."

"Certainly," I said. "Especially since I suspect it might have been staged."

Trevor cocked his head to one side and regarded me with curiosity. "Staged? By whom, and for what purpose?"

I shrugged. "By whom, I'm not quite sure. But as for the purpose—someone wanted to embarrass Harwood. You were probably too busy to notice that Harwood's producer got the whole thing on video."

"Ah," Trevor said. "Light begins to dawn." He smiled wolfishly. "And you think the handsome producer might have had something to do with the staging of the incident."

"It wouldn't surprise me in the least. There is no love lost there, that's for sure." I debated whether to reveal to Trevor the knowledge that Harwood was planning to dump Cliffie, but decided I didn't want to reveal how I had found out that juicy little tidbit.

"I can't imagine there's much love anywhere for Harwood, the pompous prat." Trevor made a face. "I've met quite a few writers since I've owned this bookshop, and except for one titled thriller writer who was the single most unpleasant ass I've ever had the misfortune to meet, Harwood is high on my list of persons never to invite back. No matter how much I might gain from having him here. He's too much trouble and much too annoying for it to be worth it. Life's too short."

"I've seen the dear man at work," I said, my voice oozing sympathy. "I can only imagine how he behaved here."

"You'd have thought one of the royals was appearing here, the way that man carried on. He quite fancies himself, no doubt about that."

"Yes, he has a healthy respect for his own worth." I grinned. "However inflated that might be."

Trevor laughed. "Despite the fact that green paint got flung all over my carpet, I must say it was worth it to see Harwood get a bit of comeuppance."

I glanced over at the spot where the paint had been thrown. There was no sign of it now. "Someone did an expert job at cleaning it up."

"I will give them that," Trevor said. "Harwood's assistant, Limpley, made sure that he gave me enough money to have it taken care of. I don't think they wanted me making a fuss." He frowned. "I wanted to call in our local bobby, but they insisted that it be kept quiet."

"Not exactly the kind of publicity that Harwood would welcome," I said.

"No," Trevor agreed. "But I should have thought they would be a bit more concerned about the incident. I overheard them talking, Harwood and Limpley, when they thought they were alone." Trevor frowned. "I gathered that this was not the first such incident. Harwood has been plagued recently with various assaults like this."

"Interesting," I said. "I wonder if someone is working up to something more extreme?"

Trevor laughed. "Just what you need, Simon. Another dead body to stumble over. Before you know it, this village will have the highest murder rate in the kingdom."

"Very funny," I said, refusing to acknowledge the appositeness of Trevor's humorous remarks. "I think perhaps it's time for me to go home and get back to work."

Trevor's hearty laughter rang in my ears as I left the bookshop and stalked back down the lane toward Laurel Cottage.

Trevor might have simply been teasing me, with some justification, but I rather wished, later that evening, that he had not been so prophetic.

Chapter Nine

I spent what remained of the morning and the entire afternoon working quite happily at the computer. All the conflict I had witnessed at Blitherington Hall had set my creative juices flowing (only metaphorically, you must realize), and I had sat down at the computer feeling quite energized. I had been thinking about a new pen name, one which I would use for a series of cozy mysteries, and the events of the past few days had given me some ideas for Diana Dorchester's first foray into crime.

By the time I realized that I must stop work in order to get ready for dinner at Blitherington Hall, I had sketched out the plot, made lists of the characters, their traits, appearance, and motives, and knocked out two rough chapters. There's nothing more satisfying than writing when one hits a streak of inspiration like this.

A glance at the clock, however, warned me that I must stop if I wanted to present myself at Blitherington Hall on time. Reluctantly I shut down the computer and filed away the pages I had printed. Taking the stairs two at a time, I went into the bathroom to take my evening pill, only half an hour late.

Ten minutes later I was correctly attired. Lady Prunella was a stickler for evening dress, and I really didn't mind indulging her, in this at least. I could say, with all honesty, that my black suit only enhanced a rather saturnine appearance, admiring the effect in my mirror (yes, we can see our reflections—it's only Hollywood nonsense that we can't.)

The Jag purred along the quiet village High Street as I made my way toward Blitherington Hall. Had the evening not been more than a bit damp, and I not on the edge of being a tad late, I might have walked. The walk from Laurel Cottage to Giles's estate was not a long one, and I was feeling restless enough at the moment to have welcomed the physical exertion.

But I didn't want to appear for dinner wet and bedraggled, not to mention late, hence the Jag. I parked in the forecourt of the Hall and retrieved an umbrella from the back seat. I could have made a dash to the front door, but I preferred a more stately approach.

I raised the knocker and let it fall, and in a moment Thompson opened the door. Standing aside, he waited for me to enter.

"Good evening, Thompson," I said, furling the umbrella and passing it over to him.

"Good evening, Professor," he said, taking the umbrella and tucking it in the crook of his arm in absent-minded fashion. "Sir Giles and Lady Prunella await you in the library."

"The library? Of course, the drawing room is still off limits, isn't it?" I smiled.

Thompson nodded, then tottered off, my umbrella dangling, forgotten, from his arm. I followed him to the library, where he opened the door to announce my presence.

The quiet hum of conversation paused only for a moment as I stepped into the room. Giles stood with his mother and Cliff Weatherstone near his desk, while Piers Limpley, Dittany Harwood, and Moira Rhys-Morgan huddled together on a sofa on the other side of the room.

"Good evening, Lady Prunella, Giles," I said. "Weatherstone." The latter, I was pleased to note, looked decidedly underdressed in a sports jacket and a shirt with no tie. Lady Prunella regarded him with disfavor. Giles, on the other hand, looked quite distinguished in his evening dress. The boy really was becoming more polished and sophisticated.

Lady Prunella noted my appearance and beamed at me. "Good evening, Simon," she said, and I almost fell backward with the shock. I couldn't remember her ever having addressed me by my first name before. "I am delighted that *you* were able to join us this evening." The not-so-subtle emphasis on the word "you" amused me, especially as I noticed Weatherstone react to it. He moved a few steps away from Lady Prunella and Giles.

"Dear lady," I said, "as ever it gives me *great* pleasure to be invited to dine at Blitherington Hall."

The wattage of Lady Prunella's answering smile left little doubt that my stock was riding high at the moment. Weatherstone stalked off to sulk by himself in the corner. Giles paid no attention to him; instead, he smiled his own greeting at me.

"Good evening, Simon," he said. "We shall go in to dinner as soon as Mr. Harwood deigns to join us."

He had raised his voice slightly, but the trio on the sofa either did not hear him or chose not to acknowledge what he had said. I glanced at my watch. It was ten minutes past eight, so Harwood was not unpardonably late, but Lady Prunella was a stickler for punctuality. If we were lucky, however, Harwood might have decided to dine in his room.

As I chatted with Giles and Lady Prunella about various innocuous village affairs, I kept my eye on Weatherstone and the rest of Harwood's entourage. Weatherstone kept to his corner, manifestly ignoring us all, while Limpley, Miss Harwood, and Mrs. Rhys-Morgan continued to whisper, in some agitation, amongst themselves.

While Lady Prunella nattered on about something to do with the flower rota at St. Ethelwold's Church, I tuned my ear toward the conversation on the sofa.

"Tomorrow," Piers Limpley was saying, "we must avoid confrontation at all costs. Whatever you do, Dittany, my dear, stay out of Zeke's way. The situation must simply *not* get any more out of hand than it already is. Zeke was in such a temper this afternoon, there's no telling what he might do."

"Frankly, Piers," Dittany hissed back at him, "I don't give a rat's arse what Zeke does, at this point. I tell you, I have had it up to here"—she gestured with her left hand somewhere above her head—"with his tantrums and his insults. He is impossible to work with. I'm thinking of going back to London tomorrow. You can all get along perfectly well without me."

"Oh, no, Dittany," Moira Rhys-Morgan said, distressed. "Please don't talk like that. You know how it would upset Zeke if you weren't here. He does rely, after all, on your color sense. He won't admit it, the poor dear, but that is the one area in which he always defers to your good taste."

"Don't *you* think so, Simon?" Lady Prunella said, claiming my attention.

I had no idea what she had just said to me, and I glanced at Giles for a clue. He had realized, clever boy that he was, that I had not been paying attention to his mother's meanderings, and he waited a moment to see what I would do. Then, taking pity on me, he responded, "Now, Mummy, you know it isn't cricket to ask Simon to try to coerce Letty Butler-Melville on your behalf in such matters. He can't spend his time running back and forth between the two of you, like some diplomat working on rapprochement between nations at war."

"Really, Giles," his mother huffed, "you *do* sometimes tend to exaggerate things unreasonably."

I smiled to ease the sudden tension. "Nevertheless, dear lady, Giles is correct. It would never do for me to interfere in such matters. I should not want you, nor the vicar's good lady, ever to despise me. Besides, I must, as ever, yield to your expertise."

Somewhat mollified, Lady Prunella paused to give it some thought. I glanced at my watch again; it was nearly eight-thirty.

Where was the wretched man? I wondered. How much longer must we wait for him?

Giles must have been thinking along the same lines, for he too checked the time. "I say, Limpley," he called to Harwood's assistant, "where the devil can Harwood be? We should go in to dinner before Cook has to put everything back in the oven."

Piers Limpley rose from the sofa. "I beg your pardon, Sir Giles," he said. "I suppose we have all quite lost track of the time. I can't think where Zeke might be. I spoke to him around seven-thirty, in his room, and he was already dressed for dinner. I reminded him of the time, and he assured me he had not forgotten." He shrugged.

Moira Rhys-Morgan frowned. "I spoke to him a few moments before that," she said. "I believe it was his intention to check something in the drawing room before joining us here."

"That was a bit over an hour ago," Giles pointed out.

Dittany Harwood emitted a snort. "Then he's probably still in the drawing room, tinkering with something. Sometimes he simply loses track of time, especially if he gets an idea to change something." She stood up. "I suppose I should go and tell him that we're going in to dinner."

"No, no, dear," Moira Rhys-Morgan said, getting up from the sofa in a hurry. "Let me do that." She turned toward Giles and Lady Prunella. "I beg your pardon, Sir Giles, Lady Prunella. I'll see what is keeping Zeke, and we'll be right along."

She hurried out the door, and the rest of us followed her at a leisurely pace, proceeding through the hall to the doors of the dining room, not far from the drawing room. Mrs. Rhys-Morgan had paused to try the doors of the drawing room, but finding them locked, she knocked and called out, "Zeke! Let me in."

She waited, then knocked again. Moments passed, but there was no response. As we all watched in silence, she headed for the front door.

"Wait, Mrs. Rhys-Morgan," I called, and she paused. "It's probably still raining. No need to go out and get wet." I turned to Giles. "Who has the key?"

"Harwood, most likely," Giles said. "He insisted that we turn over any keys to him. Limpley, do you have the key?"

Limpley shook his head. "No."

"Is there no duplicate key somewhere?" I asked Giles.

"There is a master key," Giles said. "Thompson has it." He strode over to a bellpull near the door leading to the servants' quarters and the kitchen and pulled it. A few moments later, Thompson came through the door.

"Yes, Sir Giles?" he said.

"The master key, Thompson," Giles said. "Do you have it with you? We need to open the doors to the drawing room. Mr. Harwood seems to have disappeared."

"Quite, sir," Thompson said, as if missing guests were

an everyday occurrence at Blitherington Hall. "If you will give me a moment, sir, I shall retrieve the key."

"Of course," Giles said. "We shall await you here."

No one said a word as we waited for Thompson to return with the master key. I could sense, however, that someone in the group was humming almost like an electric wire with anticipation. Limpley, Dittany, Mrs. Rhys-Morgan and Weatherstone all stood close together, in a clump, and I couldn't isolate which one of them was emanating such tension. Body language gave no one away.

At last Thompson returned with the key, and Giles almost snatched it from his hand. I was close upon Giles's heels as he inserted the key into the lock and twisted it. Opening the door, he stepped inside the drawing room. I was right behind. Before either Giles or I could make sense of what we were seeing, the others had crowded in behind us.

A collective gasp issued from those standing behind me. Then Moira Rhys-Morgan began to scream.

Chapter Ten

An arresting tableau met our horrified eyes. The room was still in considerable disarray from the efforts at redecorating, but there was an oasis of deadly order amidst the confusion. Zeke Harwood sat upon Lady Prunella's best sofa, the one piece of furniture I remembered seeing still in the room earlier in the day. He was carefully arranged in death to appear as if he were enjoying an audience with a dowager duchess.

The murderer, apparently not content with a careful arrangement of the corpse, had daubed Harwood's face and hands with the red paint that had earlier caused Lady Prunella such distress. The red contrasted sharply with the dark blue of Harwood's suit, and the murderer had dripped red paint in strange designs all over the garment.

Harwood's legs were demurely crossed at the ankles. A long swatch of fabric lay draped across the sofa next to the body. One red hand caressed it, as if Harwood were pointing out its virtues to his hostess.

Moira Rhys-Morgan had ceased screaming and begun whimpering instead. Two bodies pushed past Giles and me and approached the corpse. Piers Limpley and Dittany Harwood went to render aid to their fallen leader. Moira Rhys-Morgan quickly joined them. Alas, I knew they were too late. Harwood was beyond any human help now. I know dead people when I see them.

Before either Giles or I could stop them, Limpley and Miss Harwood were attempting in vain to rouse Harwood, clasping his hands and checking for a pulse. Mrs. Rhys-Morgan, standing between them, reached out to touch the dead man's face. Cliff Weatherstone quickly joined them, attempting to draw Mrs. Rhys-Morgan away. Lady Prunella chose that moment to launch into hysterics herself, calling our attention to something that had previously escaped our notice.

"The wall! Look at the wall!" Lady Prunella wailed. Someone—the murderer, perhaps? Or the victim?—had begun to paint one of the walls with the same red paint that now decorated the corpse.

While Giles turned to his mother, I moved forward to stop the others from disturbing the scene any further. "Step away from there," I ordered them in a loud, firm voice. Starting with surprise, they did as they were bade. Harwood's hands dropped down at his sides. I'd have to remember their original position in order to inform the police.

Piers Limpley was about to protest, but I cut him off. "There's nothing you can do for him now," I said. "He's beyond your help. We must leave him as he is, and summon the police. It's a matter for them now."

"Police?" Limpley squeaked out the word.

"Oh, Piers, don't be an idiot," Dittany said, not bothering to hide her withering contempt. "You don't think Zeke painted himself and then committed suicide, surely? Obviously someone did this to him." Suddenly overcome, she turned away.

"Oh, my poor dear Zeke," Moira Rhys-Morgan said,

her voice husky with the tears she had been shedding. "What monster did this to you?" She turned and hid her face in Cliff Weatherstone's comforting shoulder.

"All of you, please come out of the room *now,*" I said, once again raising my voice. Giles led his mother out of the room, having at last succeeded in getting her to stop babbling about the red paint on the walls. Cliff Weatherstone shot me a look of extreme dislike, but he took Moira Rhys-Morgan gently by the arm and escorted her from the room. Limpley and Dittany followed them, the latter glancing back over her shoulder one last time before I shut the door behind us.

Giles had left his mother in order to get to the telephone and summon the police. "We might as well go into the dining room," I said, moving forward to escort Lady Prunella. "If nothing else, we could all do with a stiff drink while we wait for the authorities to arrive."

I tugged an unresponsive Lady Prunella along with me, and the others trailed behind, unprotesting. Thompson appeared on cue as I seated Lady Prunella at her accustomed place, and the others found chairs and sat down. "Brandy for everyone, I think, Thompson," I instructed the butler.

"Very good, sir," Thompson said, as if nothing untoward had occurred. "And I shall instruct Cook to hold back dinner."

Giles came in, and I beckoned him to my side. "Do you have the key, Giles? We should lock the door until the police arrive."

He patted his trouser pocket. "Already done, Simon." He expelled a long breath. "What a disaster." He leaned closer. "Who do you think did it?"

We both glanced around the table at the assembled company. With the exception of Moira Rhys-Morgan, quietly sniffling into a handkerchief, no one appeared to be mourning Harwood's demise. Limpley, Dittany, and Weatherstone had all taken up their linen napkins from the table to wipe ineffectually at the red paint on their hands.

The paint on the corpse was still tacky, and if one of the three of them was the murderer, it had been quite clever to get hands on the body in order to explain any stray daubs of paint.

I thought back to our time in the library, before we had discovered the corpse. Had anyone displayed telltale signs of red paint? Not that I could recall.

With the doors to the drawing room locked, I wondered how the murderer had gained access to Harwood. Through the French windows from the terrace, of course.

I leaned toward Giles. "Did you happen to notice whether the French windows were open?"

Giles shook his head. "I'm afraid I never noticed them, Simon."

"That must be how the murderer got in and out. There's no other way."

Giles gave me an odd look. "Perhaps one of us should go take a quick look."

I thought it over. "Better not," I said. "We can't take the risk that one of these people would report it to the police. As it is, I've no doubt they'll all be loudly protesting their innocence. After all, why would one of them want to kill Harwood?"

"Other than the fact that he was a right bastard, you mean?"

The dark humor in Giles's query made me smile. "One of them has to have done it. Unless, of course, someone came in from outside through the French windows. In that case, anyone could have done it."

Thompson entered the room, bringing with him the village bobby, the rather aptly named Police Constable Peter Plodd. Dear Plodd would never win any prizes for quick thinking, but he did know his procedure. "Evening, your ladyship, Sir Giles." He made a respectful bow in the direction of Lady Prunella. "Ladies, gentlemen. If you'll all remain seated here, and no talking about what you've seen, please. Detective Inspector Chase and his team are on the way."

"Arrest this woman!" Moira Rhys-Morgan pushed back her chair so hard it fell over with a great thump. She waved a finger in the direction of Lady Prunella. "She did it! She threatened poor Zeke. Everyone heard her." Then, overcome with emotion, she covered her face with her hands and commenced sobbing.

Plodd cleared his throat as he eyed the wailing woman with great distaste. "If you please, madam, do try to calm yourself. You'll get your chance to speak to the officer in charge."

Weatherstone, who seemed to have appointed himself as Mrs. Rhys-Morgan's attendant, righted her chair and encouraged her gently to sit down again. He kept patting her arm reassuringly, and her sobs decreased in volume, if not in quantity.

As one would have expected, Lady Prunella wore a look of extreme affront, but wisely, for once, she kept quiet. She did sniff rather loudly, however.

Thus we sat in uneasy silence for another ten minutes or so, until Thompson ushered into the dining room the handsome detective inspector. Robin Chase took one look at the assembled company, then his eyes came to rest on Yours Truly. I would have been willing to swear I saw him mouth the words "I might have known."

He introduced himself and his subordinate, Detective Sergeant Harper. "I regret I must ask you all to remain here a while longer. After I have had a chance to inspect the scene, I shall want to speak with each of you in turn."

"You are welcome to use the library, Detective Inspector,"

Giles offered, his voice cool. There was little love lost between the two, because Giles was well aware how attractive I found our ace homicide detective.

"Thank you, Sir Giles," Robin said. "Your assistance is greatly appreciated." With that he turned and left the room, Harper close upon his heels. Plodd remained at his post.

Again the uneasy silence fell. Mrs. Rhys-Morgan had finally stopped her crying. I took my time and examined each of Harwood's little retinue in turn. I tried to get a reading on the emotional state of each, but there was such turmoil in the room, all the vibes were difficult to separate. Someone in the room was, however, quite pleased with him- or herself, that much I could discern. But overlaying that pleasure in a task accomplished was the fear of discovery.

Which one of them? I wondered. Mrs. Rhys-Morgan continued to be the only one of the four who appeared to be grieving, but she might well be a good actress, putting on a show for the benefit of us all. Had she really loved Harwood? She wouldn't be the first woman to have fallen hopelessly for a gay man. Perhaps she had finally snapped, thinking that if she couldn't have him, no one would. Lady Prunella would make a convenient scapegoat.

Weatherstone also had his reasons for hating Harwood. He had been, no doubt, a significant part of Harwood's success here in England, but he wasn't going along for the ride in the States. He could have decided to take the ultimate revenge for being left behind.

Piers Limpley seemed devoted to Harwood and his interests. But Harwood had hardly treated him with respect. Maybe the worm had turned.

Dittany Harwood also had evinced little love for her brother, judging by the nasty scene I had witnessed earlier in the day. She had hinted at family secrets that would embarrass Harwood. If she could have riled him that way, would she have chosen to murder him instead?

Or had someone from outside Blitherington Hall sneaked in through the French windows and killed Harwood? It could have been the person who dumped green paint all over him at the event at the bookshop.

Such speculation was useless at the moment. Until I knew more about how the murderer got in and out of the room, I couldn't do much about narrowing down the list of suspects. Giles and Lady Prunella I dismissed automatically. Neither of them had any real reason to kill Harwood. Lady Prunella had been enraged over Harwood's behavior, but she would never forget herself and her station so far as actually to commit murder.

Everyone had grown quite restive by the time Robin Chase returned. We all looked up expectantly as he entered the room and cleared his throat.

"I have completed a preliminary investigation, and it is quite clear that we are dealing with death under suspicious circumstances. I will now ask you to continue to wait, as I talk to each of you in turn. After I have spoken with you, I would ask that you retire to your rooms and stay out of the way of our investigation for the time being."

Everyone nodded. Robin glanced at me. "Dr. Kirby-Jones, if you would be so good as to join me in the library." He turned and walked out of the dining room.

I inclined my head at Lady Prunella, who was so sunk in gloom that she failed to notice. Giles raised one eyebrow in a sardonic gesture, and I winked at him. He turned his head away.

In the library, Robin had divested himself of his overcoat and sat down behind Giles's desk.

I approached the desk and sat in the chair he indicated.

Harper sat discreetly to one side, notebook and pen at the ready.

"You're looking well, Detective Inspector," I said.

Robin twitched at his moustache, something he was prone to do whenever he spent any time with me.

"Thank you, Dr. Kirby-Jones." He glanced down at something on the desk. "Might I say that I am not surprised to find you here?"

"I thought you might not be," I said demurely. "Once again I do seem to be johnny-on-the-spot."

"Quite," Robin said. "I'm sure I can rely on your skills of observation once again, Simon."

"Naturally, Robin," I said. "Now, what can I tell you?"

"Describe for me what happened when you discovered the body."

I launched into my report. I began with the time we spent waiting in vain for Harwood in the library, then moved on to our actual discovery of the body in the drawing room.

Robin made no comment until I had finished. "Four persons approached the body and actually laid their hands upon it? Mr. Piers Limpley, Miss Dittany Harwood, Mrs. Moira Rhys-Morgan, and Mr. Cliff Weatherstone, correct?"

"Yes," I said. "And afterwards they were all trying to get the red paint off their hands."

Robin had no need for me to explain the implications.

"Was the drawing room door kept locked?" Robin continued.

"Harwood was quite insistent about that," I explained. "He didn't want anyone except members of his crew seeing what they were doing, until all the work was finished." I paused. "They used the French windows leading onto the terrace to go in and out of the room."

I waited for a moment, but Robin did not respond. "Which makes me wonder, of course, whether the murderer got in and out of the room through the French windows, given that the drawing room door was kept locked."

Robin drew a deep breath. "This is to go no further for the moment, Simon." He paused.

"Of course not, Robin. You may trust me, as you have in the past."

"The French windows were locked from the inside. Furthermore, we found the key to the drawing room door in the victim's jacket pocket."

Chapter Eleven

Well, well. Shades of John Dickson Carr—a locked room puzzle! I voiced the thought to Robin, who rewarded me with a blank look.

"Carr was one of the classic writers of the Golden Age detective story," I explained. "His specialty was the locked room puzzle. You know, the kind of murder story in which the corpse is found in a locked room, where no one could get in or out, and it was seemingly impossible for the murder to have been committed." I smiled. "Naturally, there *was* a way, usually a most ingenious, if not totally believable, way. Carr wrote many stories of that type."

"I see," Robin said, now appearing somewhat dazed from my flood of information.

"I've little doubt, however," I continued, "that you've already figured out how this could have been done, haven't you?"

Robin's eyes blinked at me. "Well, um, naturally, I do have my own theory about it, Simon, but why don't you tell me yours?"

I took care not to smile this time. "Remember I told you

that four people approached the victim and attempted to revive him?"

Robin nodded. Then the light dawned. "And one of them put the key into the victim's jacket pocket. By Jove, Simon, I think you've got it."

Inclining my head graciously, I watched Robin with considerable amusement. "And what was your theory, Robin? Was it something different? Or had we hit upon the same notion? Great minds thinking alike, and all that."

Robin cleared his throat. "I had thought rather much the same as you, Simon."

"Good. Any hope that the forensics team will turn up fingerprints on the key?"

"It is certainly possible," Robin said. "There is also an awful lot of red paint to work with." He shook his head in disgust. "I gather our chappie is some kind of interior decorator."

I had to smile at the slight sneer in Robin's voice as he uttered the last two words. "Yes, he was an interior decorator, and quite a famous one at that. Haven't you heard of his television program, 'Très Zeke'?"

Robin's handsome brow furrowed for a moment. "Ah, yes. I've heard my sister going on about him." He grimaced. "Once she finds out I'm on this case, she'll pester the life out of me, wanting all the details."

"She won't be the only one."

"No, once the press get wind of this," Robin said gloomily, "they'll be after us constantly."

"Just think, Robin, of how famous you'll become once you've solved this case." I grinned at him. "The media will love you. A handsome, very photogenic police detective, and a murdered celebrity. You'll be sure to get a promotion out of this."

Detective Sergeant Harper seemed suddenly overcome by a fit of coughing. I had almost forgotten he was in the room with us. Robin cast him a severe look, and Harper's cough cleared up right away.

"That's as may be," Robin said, his tone severe. "But for now, Simon, what else can you tell me about the situation here?"

I had plenty to tell him, but I tried to keep to the essentials. Even with my editing out what seemed to be extraneous details, it still took me twenty minutes to tell it all. He appeared a bit dazed when I had finished.

"Thank you, Simon," Robin said. "That gives me quite a lot of information to be going on with." He stood up, dismissing me. "Now I simply have to determine which of them did it, and why."

"What about how?" I asked as I too stood.

Robin glanced at Harper, then back at me. He expelled a deep breath. "This is to go no further for the moment, Simon." I nodded. "It was a blow with the proverbial blunt instrument, to the back of the head. Or rather, several blows, in this case." He shook his head. "Rather dodgy, but based on what I could see, he was hit several times. We'll have to wait for the postmortem for complete information, naturally."

"Sounds like our chappie was a bit angry with poor old Zeke, then," I said. "Several blows would indicate that, don't you think?"

Robin nodded. "It's very likely. Thus, among other things, we must find out who was angry with the victim shortly before he was killed. If this was not premeditated, that is."

"I'll certainly do my best," I said, flashing Robin one of my most winning smiles.

"Now, Simon," he said, his voice taking on a peremptory tone. "I do appreciate your information, but you must be careful about getting yourself involved in my investigation."

I projected an air of hurt innocence. "Robin, naturally I would not think of interfering with your investigation. But I would certainly consider it my duty to share with you any tidbits of information I might happen to stumble across. I know you would expect no less of me."

Harper once again was overcome by a fit of coughing, and Robin simply stood and stared at me. I smiled and walked out the door.

Now what to do? I thought. Since I was not staying at Blitherington Hall like everyone else, I couldn't be expected to go up to my room until the police had finished questioning everyone. And I certainly didn't want to go home to Laurel Cottage just now.

As I stood there in the hallway, hovering indecisively, Detective Sergeant Harper came out of the library. He stopped and stared at me. "Was there something you needed, Dr. Kirby-Jones?"

I started. I so rarely had heard Harper say anything, I was not accustomed to his voice. I had forgotten how deep and rumbling it was, rather odd for such a slight man.

"Oh, nothing, Sergeant Harper," I said. "I was just wondering whether I should take my leave of my host and hostess and run off home to Laurel Cottage."

Harper frowned. "Detective Inspector Chase would prefer it if you didn't talk with anyone else involved in the case just yet."

"Of course," I said. I would have to yield as gracefully as possible and go home, despite my raging curiosity. "Then I shall bid you good evening, Sergeant Harper."

"Good evening, sir," he said, following me down the hallway.

As I passed the drawing room, I could hear sounds from inside, as the scene-of-the-crime team continued with its work of gathering evidence. I paused at the front door to look back, and saw that Harper had gone to the dining room to summon the next person for questioning. I lingered a moment to see Giles emerge from the dining room, preceded by Harper.

Giles saw me and made a quick gesture with his right hand, holding it up like a telephone receiver to his ear. I took that to mean that he would call me as soon as he had the opportunity. I nodded to show that I had understood, then let myself out the front door.

Blinking and allowing my eyes a moment to adjust to the darkness, I examined the scene. There were several additional cars and one van parked in the forecourt of Blitherington Hall, all belonging to the various members of the police and the investigative team. I strode across to where my Jag was parked, then stopped and frowned.

I couldn't go anywhere at the moment, not unless I could lift the Jag from where it was, wedged in between two other cars, and set it down in a clear area.

This was a fine little situation. I couldn't go home, and I couldn't hang around inside, hoping to nose out more information. I could always go in and explain the situation to Robin, and surely he would have someone come and help me get my car out.

How annoying. I stood there a moment longer, wavering, then made up my mind that I would simply have to risk Robin's irritation and ask him to have the cars moved.

A sudden, small movement in the shadows along the side of the house caught my eye. I stood very still. The forecourt of Blitherington Hall was not very well lit, and only someone with keen eyesight like mine would have detected anything among the shadows.

There it was again, a subtle movement. Whatever it was, it was too big to be a dog or a cat. I focused for a moment to get some kind of emotional reading, and I could detect excitement and fear in equal measure. The shadow belonged to a human being, and one who was definitely somewhere he or she should not be. A member of the police investigative team would not be lurking about in the shadows in the first place, nor would he or she be reeking of such strong emotion.

Had whoever it was seen me? I thought perhaps not. The police van was one of the vehicles blocking my Jag, and I was standing in the shadow of the van, away from the side of the house where someone hid in the bushes. I had a good view of the side of the house, but I didn't think whoever it was could see me.

I waited, my senses alert, to see what would happen next. Should I try to apprehend this person and turn him over to the police? What on earth could this person be doing, hiding in the bushes like this? Could this be the murderer, still hanging around the scene of the crime?

If that were the case, it meant that someone from outside Blitherington Hall had killed Zeke Harwood.

As I waited, the shadow got bolder. I could hear the bushes rustling now, because the night around us was still. I risked craning my neck around the edge of the van, and I caught a flash of light-colored material in the bushes. The shadow was making slow but careful progress toward the French windows, now only about three feet away.

I waited until the lurker had nearly reached the French windows before I began my own stealthy movements in the same direction. The lurker was so intent on his own goal that he did not hear my approach.

The nearer I came to the lurker, the closer he came to the French windows. By the time I was less than six feet away from him, he—or rather, she, as I could now see—was peering cautiously around the edge of the door, spying on the scene-of-the-crime team at work.

I cleared my throat, and the lurker started violently. "Good evening, Mrs. Cholmondley-Pease. Lovely night for a stroll, wouldn't you say?"

Chapter Twelve

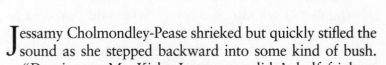

Jessamy Cholmondley-Pease shrieked but quickly stifled the sound as she stepped backward into some kind of bush.

"Dearie me, Mr. Kirby-Jones, you didn't half frighten me." She stepped out of the bush and attempted to act as if there were nothing untoward in her behavior.

"I deeply regret having frightened you, dear lady," I said in my most courtly manner, "and heaven forfend that I should appear in the least *rude* by expressing the thought, but what, might I ask, are you doing here in the bushes?"

Her eyes glazed over a bit as I spoke; regrettably, our Jessamy appeared to have trouble following the syntax of a complex sentence. Nonetheless, after a moment's stiff cogitation she managed to decipher what I had said into language she could understand. She emitted a laugh that, no doubt, she considered quite fetching, but to my ears sounded like cats involved in a certain procreative process. I winced.

"Oh, Mr. Kirby-Jones, you are a right caution. What am I doing here in the bushes?" She laughed again. I expressed the fervent wish, silently, that she would forbear to do it again.

I could see she was struggling to find an answer to my question. "Yes, what were you doing in the bushes here? You cannot have failed to notice that the police are here."

Her head, wrapped in a dark scarf, bobbed up and down. Her ensemble, except for a cream-colored blouse, was black. Some dire need had compelled her to attire herself in something other than her signature fashion statement of leopard skin. Could that dire need have been sneaking into Blitherington Hall and bashing old Harwood on the bean?

She must have read something of my thoughts from my expression, for her mouth twisted in a grimace of denial. "I didn't kill him, if that's what you're thinking!"

"Didn't kill whom?" I asked. "Who said anyone had been killed?"

Our Jessamy had never played chess, I was certain. She had led herself blindly into that trap.

"Um, er, well, I couldn't help taking a butcher's into the drawing room just now, and it's plain as the nose on me face, Mr. Harwood's dead."

I noted with interest how Jessamy's accent degenerated under stress. She was forgetting to strive for the posher-sounding tones she normally affected.

From beneath her fluttering eyelashes, she regarded me with hope. I stepped cautiously around her and peered in through the French windows, trusting that I would escape the notice of the police. Robin would not be pleased if I were caught snooping like this.

I ascertained quickly that one could, if one peered in at the correct angle, see the sofa upon which Harwood's earthly shell still sat in repose. The scene-of-the-crime team pottered about, doing whatever it was they did, and no one seemed to be paying attention to the French windows. I stepped back.

"I concede," I said, my tone severe, "that you can see

the body from here, and even identify it. But that still doesn't answer my original question. What were you doing here in the bushes?"

The moment I had taken to peer within the drawing room had given her just the bit of breathing space she needed to marshal her thoughts, meager as they might be. She smiled at me, no doubt hoping to entice my admiration to such an extent that I would believe whatever lie she was about to utter.

As I waited for her to speak, I glanced down at her neck. Faint light from the French windows glowed across said body part while the rest of her was veiled in shadow. The pulsing of the blood in that vein seemed to be calling to me. Transfixed by the sight of that beautiful, delicious vein, I heard an odd roaring in my ears.

Jessamy said something, but I made no sense of it. That lovely vein claimed all my attention, and without volition my lips parted and my head began to lower toward it. Jessamy expelled a breath and said something else, even as she stepped closer. All I could think about was how incredibly wonderful it would be to press my lips against that throbbing portal of pleasure. I shuddered and brought my lips ever closer.

The squeak of the French windows as they opened brought me back to my senses, and with a muffled squeak Jessamy drew her scarf around her neck and bolted through the bushes.

I stood there, blinking, like the complete ass I suddenly felt myself to be, as one of the scene-of-the-crime personnel stepped through the French windows onto the terrace.

Wishing for once that I could draw in a deep breath to steady myself, I stared at the startled woman.

"Excuse me, sir," she said sternly, "but I'm afraid I'll have to ask you to stand away from here. There is an investigation going on, and you shouldn't be here."

"Ah, yes, I do realize that," I said, as my brain once again began to do its business. "Detective Inspector Chase has taken my statement and dismissed me, but my car is blocked in. I was just coming to ask whether someone might be able to let me out."

"Oh, I see," she said, following the direction indicated by my outstretched arm and pointing finger. "Half a mo." She stepped back inside the drawing room.

I turned around to scan the immediate area, but Jessamy Cholmondley-Pease had made good her escape. I could see nothing moving in the shadows, nor could I sense her presence anywhere nearby. She had done a runner, and if she had any sense, she was halfway to the village by now.

She had achieved only a brief respite, I resolved, for I would catch up with her as soon as I could and get the truth out of her. I supposed I should let Robin know I had found her hanging about outside, and I would, in due time.

A few minutes later, when the vans had been moved, my Jag had room to maneuver, and I settled myself inside, ready for the short drive home.

What on earth was wrong with me? I asked myself as I negotiated the turns required to get my Jag out of its parking space and down the lane away from Blitherington Hall. Why this sudden fascination with veins in the neck? And the neck of Jessamy Cholmondley-Pease, of all people? I shuddered. I had never fancied women while I was alive and breathing, and I wasn't about to start now. Death hadn't made me suddenly bisexual.

Or at least I didn't think it had. Perhaps it was a side effect of my pills. No one had ever warned me this might occur. There had been a few cases of hair growing in odd places and the occasional reports of the urge to bay at the moon, but nothing like this.

Upon reflection, I decided I had much rather go bay at the moon.

Within minutes I had parked the Jag at Laurel Cottage and let myself in. I was far too rattled by what had occurred between me and Jessamy to be able to settle down to write, which is what I would have done any other time.

I glanced at my watch, calculating the time difference between here and Houston, Texas. If I were lucky, I might just catch Tristan Lovelace, professor of medieval history and ever-so-dashing vampire, in his office at the university where he taught.

Tristan had had the distinct honor of inducting Yours Truly into the union, as it were. I had fallen madly in love with my graduate advisor, and for a time he had returned my passion, even to the extent of confiding his deep, dark secret. Though at first I was repelled by what he told me, eventually I came to the decision that becoming a vampire was far less risky than other things that might befall me. And thus I was initiated.

Alas for my hopes of happily-ever-after with Tris, however. He was a man of voracious appetites, and soon his predilection for me faded. He had, however, felt abashed enough about dumping me that he had gifted me with Laurel Cottage, hence my residence in Snupperton Mumsley.

All of the above being a rather long explanation for why I decided to consult Tris. If anyone knew why my pills had suddenly gone wonky, he would.

Luck was with me, for Tris answered straight away. "Hello, Tris," I said. "It's Simon."

"Hullo, Simon," Tris boomed back at me, and I smiled to hear the pleasure in his voice. Despite all that had happened between us, he was still genuinely very fond of me. "Hold on a moment, Simon, and I shall be able to give you my full attention."

I heard the receiver being laid upon his desk, the rustle

of papers, and Tris's voice as he dismissed whoever was in his office when his phone rang.

Then he was back. "How are you, Simon? Stumbled over any more dead bodies lately?"

"Very funny, Tris," I said sourly. "As a matter of fact, there *has* been a murder at Blitherington Hall."

"Young Giles finally cut the leading strings and bashed his barmy mother over the head?"

I detected a note of jealousy in Tris's voice as he spoke Giles's name, and I must admit to the slightest frisson of pleasure. I had confided in him Giles's pursuit of my affections, plus the fact that I was tempted to yield to said pursuit.

"Not this time," I said, laughing, "but it is a tempting thought." As quickly as I could, I sketched the scenario for him.

"Quite a bumblebroth," Tris observed, using a word that had been in vogue in his human youth. "But I've little doubt, Simon, that you shall soon have routed the murderer, and all shall be well again in the sacred confines of Blitherington Hall."

"Your faith in my abilities touches me to the very depths of my soul," I said, a trifle waspishly. "But I didn't call to tell you about the latest exercise of the little gray cells. I have a problem, and I really haven't the slightest idea what's going on."

"What is it?" Tris said, responding to the unease in my words.

"The past couple of days," I said, "I find myself suddenly wanting to bite people on the neck. Tonight I came very close to doing that very thing . . . and to a woman."

"*Quelle horreur,*" Tris said, laughing. "That *is* a problem."

"I'm so pleased that you find this amusing," I said. "But do try to suppress your amusement for the moment, and tell me, please, what the hell is going on? Why is this happening?"

"Nothing to worry about, dear boy," Tris said, turning serious. "Occasionally one gets a batch of those little pills that aren't quite tickety-boo. Just bung an extra one down the throat, and all will be right with the world. Don't waste your time worrying about it."

Much relieved, I said, "Thanks, Tris. I really was worried that I was losing my mind. No one ever warned me this could happen."

"There's no guidebook to being a member of the union," Tris said. "More's the pity, I sometimes think."

"Perhaps you should write one," I said with some asperity. Tris fancied himself as quite the authority on a number of subjects, not just his academic specialty.

"No time, Simon, no time." Tris dismissed it. "I was going to ring you up, actually."

"Oh," I said. That was a turnabout. "And why might you have been going to do that?"

"I'm going to be in England in a couple of months. I've been invited to present a lecture at Oxford, and afterwards I'll be spending some time in London for a bit of research at the British Library. I thought I might pop down for a few days' visit, if it were convenient for you."

I almost dropped the phone in my surprise. Tris, coming to visit me?

"You're certainly welcome, Tris," I said. "Any special reason for honoring me with your presence?"

He laughed. "Suspicious as ever, Simon. Actually, there is something I should like to discuss with you, but I would much prefer doing it face to face."

I froze as a horrible thought struck me. Maybe he wanted Laurel Cottage back. I couldn't bear that, but how could I refuse if he insisted? He had been incredibly generous to give it to me, but perhaps he had had second thoughts about it. If necessary, I could offer to buy it. These days, at least, I could afford it.

I suppressed my unease and discussed the date of Tris's arrival and plans for his visit. A few minutes later, he rang off, and I set the receiver down, staring at it as if it were a viper in my hand.

I shook my head. In best Scarlett O'Hara fashion, I decided, I would think about that tomorrow. For now, I would force myself to focus my attention on writing. I went upstairs to change my clothes, take another pill, and get my head in the right space for creative work. Writing was the distraction I sorely needed now.

Sometime the next morning, an hour or so after the sun had come peeping in the windows of my office, the phone rang. I picked up the receiver and stuck it in my ear. "Hello," I mumbled, my attention still focused on the computer screen.

"Simon!" Giles fairly shouted in my ear. "You must come at once. They're going to arrest my mother!"

Chapter Thirteen

Giles rang off before I could question him. I contemplated ringing him back and demanding an explanation but decided not to waste time. I hurriedly saved my work on the computer, shut the machine down, then sprinted upstairs to make myself presentable for a visit to Blitherington Hall.

Within ten minutes I was unlocking the Jag, ready to speed through the village. In contrast to the wet weather of the day before, the sun shone brightly this morning. I had provided myself with gloves, hat, and sunglasses, but even so, I felt the sun's heat more than I should. I had taken my morning pill, but perhaps I should have taken two. Reaching into my pocket, I pulled out the small bottle containing an emergency supply and tapped a pill into my hand. I swallowed it quickly. Better to be overmedicated, I decided.

A few minutes later, as I approached the lane leading to Blitherington Hall, I discovered that the press had evidently found out about the murder. There were seven or eight folk milling about, but a couple of police constables were keeping an eye on them, making sure they didn't make a dash for the house. Several cameras were pointed in my direction as I pulled the Jag up to the constable guarding the entrance to the driveway. Rolling down the window, I wished the PC a good morning and gave her my name.

She pulled a list from her pocket, scanned it, then nodded. "Go right on, Professor."

"Thank you, Constable," I said. Putting the Jag in gear again, I drove the hundred yards or so to the forecourt of Blitherington Hall, where I recognized the car Robin Chase and his sergeant usually drove. I found it difficult to believe that Robin was actually going to arrest Lady Prunella for murder. He had known the woman long enough, I should think, to realize that she would never soil her hands with something so sordid as murder.

Thompson responded to my knock immediately, as if Giles had prompted him to wait by the front door for my arrival.

"Good morning, Thompson," I said, handing him my hat and gloves. "Where is Sir Giles? He rang me just now, and he sounded rather upset."

"You'll find him in the morning room, Professor," he said, his face giving nothing away. "The inspector is speaking with her ladyship in the library just now."

"Thank you, Thompson." I strode down the hall toward the morning room. I knocked, then opened the door without waiting for a response from within.

Giles and Cliff Weatherstone were seated on one of the sofas, and Cliff had one hand on Giles's shoulder. They looked up, startled, as I burst into the room.

"I beg your pardon," I said, the frost obvious in my voice. "Perhaps I should come back later? Although I did make haste to come here, thinking you were facing some sort of dire emergency."

Giles stood up, shaking off Weatherstone's hand. "Don't

be an ass, Simon," he said waspishly. "I do need your help, otherwise I wouldn't have rung you. Cliff was merely acting as any friend would in this situation."

"And what situation is that?" I asked, not buying the explanation. Giles might think Cliff was acting in a friendly manner, but from where I stood, Cliff wanted something besides friendship from Giles. "From the rather frantic nature of your call, I expected to see Lady Prunella being led from here in chains."

"It just might come to that," Giles said, his brow darkening in irritation, "if something isn't done. I know you have all the faith in the world in your tame policeman, but I expect he would dearly love to humiliate my mother and me by charging her with this murder."

"Don't be absurd, Giles," I said sharply, dropping down into a chair across from the sofa. "I know there is little love lost between you and Detective Inspector Chase, but whatever else you might think of him, he is thoroughly professional. I rather doubt that he would charge your mother with murder simply to humiliate either of you. If he should happen to charge your mother, then he would have a darn good reason to do so."

Giles collapsed on the sofa, and Cliff patted his arm in a reassuring manner.

"I have to agree with Kirby-Jones, Giles, though it pains me to admit it," Cliff said, flashing me a look redolent with distaste. "Chase seems like a bright chap. I shouldn't think he would do such a thing lightly."

"Some consolation," Giles muttered. "It's not *your* mother about to be hauled off to chokey. And with the press waiting like vultures to report everything."

"Why are you so convinced that Lady Prunella is going to be charged?" I asked. "Do you know something about all this the police don't?"

Giles shrugged and cut his eyes sideways at Cliff. He did

know something, but he was reluctant to tell me in front of Cliff. Interesting, I thought. Perhaps Cliff wasn't on the A-list just yet.

"Why is Robin talking with your mother right now?" I asked, shifting the subject until I could think of a way to get Cliff out of the room without being too obvious.

Giles drew in a deep breath, then slowly released it. "She was seen coming out of the drawing room about a quarter hour before we met in the library before dinner."

That was not good news. "Who saw her?"

Giles shrugged. "It was an anonymous tip to the police. That's all I managed to discover before Chase took my mother into the library for further questioning. They've been in there for a bit over half an hour now," he concluded, glancing at his watch.

"Has your mother spoken to you about any of this?" I said.

"No," replied Giles.

"Surely you don't think Lady Prunella killed Harwood?" I scoffed at the idea. "She would never do such a thing."

"You know that, and I know that," Giles said, "but others might see the situation differently." He threw up his hands. "And you know how obstinate my mother is, how much upon her dignity she can get. *The very idea that Lady Prunella Blitherington should be questioned by the police!*" Giles did a fair imitation of his mother's voice, then he shook his head in disgust. "God knows what a muddle she will make of it."

"Surely she wouldn't be that stupid," Cliff said.

"Not stupid," I said. "Stubborn. She won't like having to explain herself to a mere policeman." Frankly, I had to stifle a laugh at the thought of what was going on in the library right now. The face-off between Robin and Lady Prunella would rival a scene from a farcical stage whodunit.

Taking myself to task for such mental levity in the face of Giles's distress, I asked, "Does anyone know what she was doing in the drawing room?"

"I'm not quite certain," Giles said. "I had no idea she had even been in the drawing room at all before we discovered the body."

"And no one knows whether Harwood was in there, alive or dead, when she was in the room."

"No, Simon," Giles responded.

"Then this *is* a bit of a mess, at least until we can get the story straight from the horse's mouth, so to speak." Trust Lady Prunella, I thought, to make a difficult situation even more complicated.

"Ought I to call our solicitor, Simon?" Giles asked.

"Not just yet, Giles," I said, "no point in putting the cart before the horse, and all that."

Reassured, Giles rubbed a weary hand across his forehead. "I suppose not. There must surely be some innocent explanation." He turned to Cliff. "My apologies for burdening you with all this, Cliff. It will be sorted out soon, I trust. But now, if you'll forgive me, there's something I need to discuss privately with Simon."

Cliff took affront at such a dismissal, no matter how politely couched. He smoothed the irritation out of his face and rose from the sofa. "Certainly, Giles. But if there is anything I can do to assist you, please do not hesitate to call upon me."

Nodding curtly in my direction, Cliff stalked from the room and closed the door behind him with a barely perceptible thump.

I took care not to let Giles see how pleased I was that he had got rid of Cliff. "What is it, Giles? What is there to say for my ears alone?"

Giles rubbed his forehead again. "There is something I have to decide whether to reveal to the police, Simon.

Something that could make things look very black indeed for my mother." He sighed deeply. "Of course, by now Mummy may have saved me the trouble and dug the hole even deeper."

"Oh, dear," I said. "Then you have quite a quandary before you."

"Yes, and I need your advice."

Having said so, he lapsed into silence, staring down at his hands. He was clearly torn. Not, I think, about confiding in me, but once he told me whatever it was, he knew there would be no going back.

"Do you have any idea," I asked gently to ease him into it, "why your mother would have gone to speak to Harwood in the first place?"

"That blasted red paint," Giles said bitterly. "All she could think about was Harwood painting the room red. And then of course there was that ridiculous video he had of her. She was furious about that, and I can't say that I blame her in the least."

"But how would she have gained access to the drawing room in the first place?" I asked. "Did she get the master key from Thompson? I can't imagine that Harwood would have let her into the room, given how he carried on earlier about keeping everyone but his crew out of there."

Giles sighed. "That's where my dilemma lies, Simon. I know how Mummy got into the room. She didn't need a master key."

He paused, and I could have screamed in frustration. "Don't tell me—there's a secret way into the drawing room." I said this half-jestingly, but from the unhappy expression on Giles's face, I knew I had guessed correctly.

"Oh, my," I said. "Shades of Nancy Drew and *The Hidden Staircase*. That does make things a bit sticky."

"What on earth are you yammering on about, Simon? Who is bloody Nancy Drew, and what does she have to do with anything?" Giles was not best pleased with my moment of whimsy.

"Nancy Drew is a famous girl detective in American children's books," I said, "and in one of her cases, she investigated an old house riddled with secret passages."

"You do say the oddest things sometimes, Simon," Giles complained. "If we could come back to the point at hand?"

"Certainly, Giles," I said placatingly. "I didn't mean to make light of the situation."

"The master bedroom is directly above the drawing room, and the passage is a staircase connecting the two."

"When was it built?" I asked.

"The original part of the Hall dates back to the seventeenth century," Giles said, "so I expect it had something to do with the civil war. The Blitherington of that time was a devout Royalist, but he played at Puritanism as long as Cromwell was in power, in order to keep the family fortunes intact."

"Are there any other secret rooms or passages?"

Giles nodded. "There is a secret cellar, not terribly large, and the entrance to it is from this same secret passage."

"Who else knows about the passage, besides you and your mother?"

"Thompson probably does. He's been here forever, and most likely my dear departed father confided in him." Giles considered for a moment. "Other than that, I shouldn't think anyone else knows."

"But perhaps someone found out."

"How?"

I shrugged. "We'll have to find out. It's just possible someone used it to murder Harwood, and the matter of the drawing room key in Harwood's pocket was nothing but a red herring."

Giles brightened. "That's true."

"Moreover," I continued, "the fact that Lady Prunella was seen coming out of the drawing room by the conventional means should argue in her favor."

"Ah, yes," Giles said. "I was in such a funk, I hadn't thought that through. Someone would have had to lock the door behind her, which means Harwood was still alive when she left him." Giles stood up, relief written large across his face. "Simon, I could kiss you. I knew you'd help me make sense of this bloody mess."

"Glad to be of service, as always," I said modestly. I too stood. "Now, about that kiss."

Giles smiled and moved closer. He obliged quite nicely. If I were still a breather, I do believe I should have been a bit short of breath at the conclusion of that little interlude. Giles certainly was. So much for Cliff Weatherstone!

A discreet knock sounded at the door, and Giles stepped back and straightened his tie. "Yes?" he called.

Thompson opened the door. "Beg pardon, Sir Giles, but the detective inspector wishes to talk with you in the library."

"Yes, of course," Giles said. He offered me a sweet smile as he left the room. Thompson stood aside for him, then turned to look at me.

"Professor," he said. "If you would be so kind, Lady Prunella wishes to speak with you in her sitting room."

"Certainly, Thompson."

"If you'll come with me then, Professor, I will show you the way."

I followed the butler up the stairs to the first floor and down the corridor. I had half-expected to see a police guard posted at the door of the master bedroom, but there was none. Evidently Lady Prunella had not told Robin Chase about the secret passage.

Thompson paused in front of a door across the hall from the master bedroom and knocked. Responding to a summons from within, he opened the door and announced me.

I stepped inside, where I found Lady Prunella collapsed upon a divan. Advancing toward her, I held out my hand. "My dear Lady Prunella, Giles called to tell me that the police were questioning you. I trust that you didn't find the interview too upsetting."

Lady Prunella shuddered as she clasped the proffered hand. "It was quite unpleasant, though the detective inspector behaved in a more gentlemanly manner than I had supposed he would."

Her hand was ice-cold. I patted it reassuringly. "Detective Inspector Chase is quite clever, Lady Prunella. I'm certain he will have all this sorted out quickly, and you need not worry."

"I wish I could share your confidence in the man, Simon," she said. Releasing my hand, she indicated that I should sit down in a nearby chair.

"Now, what is it that you wished to speak to me about?" I asked.

"I wish to retain your services, Simon," she said. "You *must* solve this murder before the noble name of Blitherington is *irrevocably* besmirched!"

Chapter Fourteen

I don't know which surprised me the more, the unaccustomed familiarity with which Lady Prunella had addressed me or her plea for me to play amateur detective.

"I shall certainly be more than happy to do whatever I can, Lady Prunella," I said, "but there is no need to speak of 'retaining' my services. I assure you that I would never seek any kind of remuneration for whatever assistance I might render."

I could sense her relief. The Blitheringtons were comfortable, but by no means wealthy, for the maintenance of Blitherington Hall consumed much of their income. Were I to be so uncouth as to charge Lady Prunella for what I planned to do anyway, with or without her invitation, she could not afford me.

"You are very generous, Simon," she said. "In times of *such* travail, it is *most* heartening to know that one may rely upon one's *friends.*" She beamed at me.

Dear me, I thought, *the old girl really is softening.*

"If I am to assist you, dear lady, then I am afraid we must get down to brass tacks, as they say." I regarded her kindly but sternly. "And that means, of course, that you must tell me everything. No holding anything back."

She bobbed her head up and down. "Quite. You may rely upon me, dear boy."

I sat back in my chair. "Then let us begin with the incident about which Detective Inspector Chase has just questioned you."

Lady Prunella inclined her head. "What do you wish to know, Simon?"

"Giles told me about the existence of the hidden staircase that connects the master bedroom to the drawing room. Did you make use of it last evening?"

"To my deepest and most sincere regret, I did."

"Tell me what occurred."

"I was most concerned," Lady Prunella said after a moment's pause to gather her thoughts, "about what that *wretched* man planned to do to my drawing room. I *rue* the day I ever succumbed to the *mad* idea of writing to him to invite him to Blitherington Hall. But that cannot be helped *now.*"

I waited, trying not to fidget. Getting Lady Prunella to proceed from point A to point B and so on, without digressing mightily, would be a good test of my patience.

"I had overheard Mr. Harwood tell one of his staff, Mr. Limpley, I believe, that he would be working in the drawing room on his own for a half hour or so before dinner."

"Where did you hear this? And when?" I asked.

"I was passing by Mr. Harwood's bedroom—*my* bedroom, I should say! The *nerve* of that man!—and the door was open. I could hear him quite plainly."

"And the time?" I prompted her.

"I am not completely certain," she said, "but it was perhaps half an hour, perhaps slightly more, before we were to gather in the library before dinner."

"About seven-thirty then," I said, "but maybe a few minutes before that."

"Yes," she replied.

"What did you do then?"

She studied her hands, resting in her lap. "I am not *proud* of my behavior, Simon. It ill becomes a woman of *my* stature to have behaved in such a *common* fashion, but I plead the excuse that I was so worried I *quite* forgot myself."

I kept quiet, though it was a struggle.

"After hearing that Mr. Harwood planned to work on his own for a bit," Lady Prunella went on, "I went back to my temporary quarters, rather than downstairs as I had planned. I *had* meant to consult with Thompson about something, but it *quite* slipped my mind after that." She looked wretchedly embarrassed, and I maintained an expression of concern, trying not to yield to the impulse to laugh. "I *lurked* in the doorway of my room, peering out and waiting for Mr. Limpley and Mr. Harwood to depart from the master bedroom."

"How long did you have to wait?"

"Mr. Limpley left right after I reached my room and settled myself at my vantage point. Mr. Harwood left a minute or two later."

Really, these regular pauses were beginning to get annoying. "And then?"

"I stuck my head out and looked up and down the hallway. I did not see anyone about, so I moved quickly to the door of Harwood's room and opened it. My heart was *pounding* so, I could hear nothing but the sound of my own breathing. I was nearly *overset,* I must tell you, by the shameless *audacity* of what I was about to do."

"Quite understandable under the circumstances," I assured her.

She spared me a glance of gratitude before she continued. "I opened the entrance to the secret passageway, and to my surprise, it opened quite easily. I can't *think* when someone might have used it last, and it was *always* wont to be a bit stubborn."

That point definitely bore further investigation, but I didn't want to interrupt the flow to question her about it now.

"I made my way *carefully* down the stairs," Lady Prunella went on, "and at the bottom, I paused by the door into the drawing room. There is a peephole there, and I stood for several minutes, watching for Mr. Harwood."

"How much of the room can be seen from the peephole?" I asked.

"Only a *small* portion, I fear," Lady Prunella answered. "For a few minutes at least, I caught *no* glimpse of Harwood. I could hear him moving around, but he must have been on the side of the room nearer the French windows. *That* part of the room is not visible through the peephole."

"Do you have any idea of what time it was by then?"

Lady Prunella shook her head. "I've really no *clear* idea, though I would say that it was no longer than ten minutes after I had first heard Mr. Limpley and Mr. Harwood speaking upstairs."

That would put us at about seven-forty.

"Do continue," I said.

"Mr. Harwood came into view, and he was carrying a tin of paint. I had little doubt that it was that *red* paint, and he was about to start *painting* with it." She paused, and an expression of disgust crossed her face. "I *quite* forgot myself at that point, and I *burst* out of the passageway and startled Mr. Harwood so that he dropped the tin of paint on the floor and a bit of it spilled out."

"And was it the red paint?"

She nodded. "He recovered himself quite quickly, and

he began speaking to me in the *most* offensive manner. 'What the devil do you mean, woman, popping out of the wall and frightening me like that?' I believe those were his *exact* words.

"I did not *deign* to apologize, for I believe his behavior to *me* and his actions did not warrant such a concession on *my* part. Instead, I pointed to the red paint and accused him of *deliberately* planning to ruin my drawing room with it."

"What did he say to that?"

"He *laughed* and said that there was *nothing* I could do to prevent him because of the contract we had signed. He was *most* offensive, Simon. He said a number of *derogatory* things about the decor of the room and that *anything* he did to it could only improve it. Moreover, he said that I had all the taste of a pickled herring." Her face burned with shame at the memory. "Then, I'm afraid, I *quite* forgot myself and slapped his face."

"Oh, dear," I said. "That was *most* unfortunate."

Lady Prunella detected nothing of the amusement I felt as she continued. "At that point, he used even *more* offensive language, which I would not care *ever* to repeat, had I even recognized the words! He grabbed me by the arm and *frog-marched* me to the drawing room door. He opened it, *thrust* me out of the room, and locked the door behind me." She shuddered. "It was *most* humiliating."

"That was when someone saw you and reported it anonymously to the police."

"And I *cannot* think who might have done that," Lady Prunella said, obviously puzzled. "There was, fortunately, not a *soul* in the hallway when Mr. Harwood so *viciously* thrust me out of the drawing room. *Who* could have seen it?"

I had an idea about that, but I didn't want to share it with Lady Prunella just yet.

"Let's come back to that," I said. "Once you were out in the hallway, what did you do next?"

"I collected myself," Lady Prunella answered, "and proceeded to the library, where I *indulged* myself in a spot of brandy. I do find that, on the exceedingly *rare* occasion that necessitates it, a bit of brandy does *wonders* for the state of one's nerves."

"Yes, it is quite the restorative," I said. "And after what you had just suffered, it is certainly understandable."

"I do *so* appreciate your understanding, Simon. I quite believe I have heretofore rather *misjudged* you, dear boy."

"Thank you, Lady Prunella," I said, inclining my head modestly. I decided to ignore the condescension with which she just favored me.

"How long was it before anyone else appeared in the library?" I asked.

"Several people arrived at once, just a few minutes before eight. Giles, with that young Weatherstone, who seems to be *always* hanging about him. And Mrs. Rhys-Morgan." She paused, considering. "Then Mr. Limpley and Miss Harwood came in together, and you arrived shortly after that."

I sat thinking for a moment. If the murderer were one of Harwood's associates, then the murder had taken place sometime between the time Lady Prunella had made her undignified exit from the drawing room and Limpley, Cliff, and the two women arrived in the library. That didn't allow much time for the murder to take place.

"Did you notice anything odd about any of the members of Mr. Harwood's staff?" I finally asked.

Lady Prunella shook her head. "No, I'm afraid I was still rather *shaken* by what had occurred in the drawing room. I paid *very* little attention to any of our guests."

"No matter," I said. "I shall ask Giles if he noticed anything. Now, Lady Prunella, I must ask you, did you tell everything that you've just told me to Detective Inspector Chase?"

Lady Prunella blushed. "Oh, Simon, I did *not,* but perhaps I *should* have. I find myself in the quite *absurd* position of having *lied* to the police."

"In what manner did you lie to Detective Inspector Chase?"

"I did *not* tell him the truth of how I gained entrance to the drawing room. I told him that I had knocked upon the door and that Mr. Harwood had let me in."

It would really have been easier, all round, if Lady Prunella had told Robin the truth. Her having lied only complicated matters unnecessarily, I feared. Robin would not look kindly upon her attempts to lead him astray, but before I took her to task over this point, I wanted to ask some more questions.

"Let us go back, Lady Prunella, to when you first burst—your word—into the drawing room from the secret passageway. Obviously Harwood was startled by your sudden appearance."

"Yes, he was," she acknowledged.

"I think it rather odd that he made no other remark about the existence of the secret passageway. Or did he?"

Lady Prunella was most emphatic. "No, he didn't say a *word* about it. He paid no attention to it. Even in the circumstances one would think he *might* have taken notice of it."

"If he knew about it already, he wouldn't," I said. "You also told me that when you opened the door to the passage in the master bedroom, it opened quite easily, and that normally it did not do so."

"Yes," Lady Prunella said. "Usually it made a bit of a *squeaking* noise, but this time it didn't."

"Then we must conclude that Harwood himself had already discovered the passageway," I said. "The questions are *how* and *when?*"

"Oh, dear," said Lady Prunella.

Chapter Fifteen

"What is it, Lady Prunella?" I prompted her gently. She had gone quiet and was drumming her fingers in her lap after that soft exclamation.

"It's *my* fault, I fear," she said. "You'll think me the most idiotic creature *imaginable,* Simon, for not having realized it *sooner.*"

"For not having realized what, Lady Prunella?" I tried not to get testy with her, but my patience was fraying rapidly.

"I believe that you are *quite* correct in your assumption that Mr. Harwood *knew* about the secret passageway. Oh, really, it is all *too* humiliating for words."

"What happened?"

"Earlier, in the afternoon, I could no longer *restrain* myself, Simon. I had to know *what* that *awful* man was doing in the drawing room, and I'm afraid I *sneaked* into the master bedroom when I thought they were all downstairs. I opened the door to the secret passageway, and I went down to the peephole to see what was going on."

"Did the door squeak that time when you opened it?"

"Yes, it did! I had forgotten that," she said, her eyes widening.

"How long were you at the peephole?"

"No more than five or six minutes," Lady Prunella said after thinking about it for a moment. "At that time I could see *no* signs of red paint being used, and I was *quite* relieved, I must tell you! I was *just* upon the point of going back up the stairs when I heard Mr. Harwood tell someone he must retrieve something from his room. I thought I had best stay where I was until Mr. Harwood returned to the drawing room, *then* make my way up the stairs as quickly and quietly as I could, and no one would *ever* be the wiser."

"How long was Harwood away from the drawing room?" I asked.

"Only five minutes or so. The time it took him to go upstairs, retrieve a pair of glasses from his room, and then come *right* back down again." She sighed. "I climbed the stairs, and to my utter *horror,* I found that I had left the passageway door just the *tiniest* bit ajar."

"Would it have been noticeable to someone in the bedroom?"

Lady Prunella nodded. "I believe so. Though if Mr. Harwood were in a *great* hurry, he *might* have missed it."

"When the police allow us back into the room," I said, "you'll have to show it to me, and then we'll see. But I think it very likely that he saw the opening, quickly investigated, and realized that someone might be inside. For whatever reason, he affected not to know about it . . . at least for the time being. We'll have to question the members of his staff to find out whether he mentioned it to them."

I sat and thought for a moment, while Lady Prunella waited in anxious silence. "I believe, Lady Prunella, that we should inform the police of the existence of the secret passageway."

"Oh, dear," she said, a faint tinge of red coming into her

face. "If *you* think it best, Simon, but I do so *fear* that the detective inspector will think it simply *proves* my guilt."

"No doubt Detective Inspector Chase's first reaction will be irritation, Lady Prunella," I said kindly, "but he will be quick to see the implications of your story. Though we have no other corroboration as yet that Harwood spotted the open door and might have informed his associates, I think it best if the police have their crime scene staff go over the passageway. They may well find evidence that someone besides you made use of it recently."

"I see," Lady Prunella said, appearing relieved.

"Moreover," I said, "I don't believe we should run the risk of letting any possible evidence go undetected. I know it will mean a few uncomfortable moments for you, when you 'fess up to the detective inspector. In the long run, however, it's the wisest thing to do."

"If *that* is what you advise, Simon," she said, smiling in gratitude. "I must say, I feel *ever* so much more confident with *you* assisting dear Giles and me."

"You're most welcome, Lady Prunella," I said. I was quite beginning to like the old girl; she was thawing at a rapid rate toward Yours Truly.

I stood up. "I shouldn't let any more time pass before you go to the detective inspector and amend your statement. The sooner he has his team investigate the passageway, the better."

Lady Prunella patted her hair, as if girding herself for battle. She stood, and I followed her to the door. "Would you like me to go with you, at least as far as the library?"

"That would be *most* kind of you, Simon," she said, and thus I escorted her downstairs.

I tapped on the door of the library, and in a moment, Robin's sergeant opened it and stuck his head out. "Yes?"

"Lady Prunella wishes to amend the statement that she gave Detective Inspector Chase earlier," I said.

"Just a tick," Sergeant Harper said, then closed the door.

After about five minutes, the door opened again, and Giles came out. Harper motioned for Lady Prunella to enter, and with a quick, tremulous smile at Giles and me, she went inside. The door closed behind her.

"What's going on, Simon?" Giles asked. "What is Mummy going to tell Chase?"

I glanced around. At the moment, there was no one else in the hall, but I thought it best if I informed Giles of his mother's intentions in a more private place. "Let's go back upstairs, and I'll tell you."

"Very well," Giles said, then led the way back up the stairs and down to the end of the hall to the sitting room attached to his bedroom. He closed the door behind us and motioned for me to take a seat. He sat down across from me and waited.

Succinctly I related to him what had passed between his mother and me, and though he frowned, I could see that he understood the sense of my advice to Lady Prunella.

"It's probably just as well," Giles said, sighing. "If it were to come out later, it would look much more damaging, I suppose."

"I think so," I replied. "And though we have no real proof that what your mother is telling Robin is the truth, at least at the moment, I believe his crime scene staff will find anything there is to find."

"Not to mention the fact that he can question Harwood's associates about it as well, if what you suspect is true."

"We can have a go at them as well, once Robin is through with them," I said.

Giles laughed, a bit sourly. "Despite the faith you claim to have in Chase's abilities to solve this case and to treat my mother fairly, you seem nevertheless intent upon meddling."

I took affront at that. "It didn't seem to me that you minded my *meddling,* as you call it, when you phoned me this morning and asked for my assistance."

Giles had the grace to look abashed. "Sorry, Simon, that was unworthy of me. You're right. I did ask for your help, and I'm very grateful for it. Chase rather got up my nose just now. He seems to dislike me. For whatever reason, I rub him the wrong way." He grinned. "And it's mutual."

"I've little doubt that it's because you've made it painfully obvious that you don't like him," I said severely.

"I can't help it if I'm jealous," Giles said, taking affront. "The way you look at him, Simon, honestly, it's enough to drive anyone mad."

"Just because I look at an attractive man with interest doesn't necessarily mean anything, Giles," I said with asperity. "Were I to stoop so low, I might mention that I have seen you do the same thing, most particularly with one Cliff Weatherstone."

Giles laughed. "Guilty as charged, Simon."

I thought it best to change the subject. "I do wish I could examine this secret passageway, but I suppose we'll have to wait until the police are finished with it. I wouldn't want to risk contaminating any evidence they might find. Robin would be livid."

"No doubt," Giles said. "But, honestly, there's not much to see. It's not terribly interesting. I played in it sometimes as a child, and once I locked my loopy sister in it for three hours when she was being particularly annoying."

"Where is Alsatia, by the way?"

Giles snorted. "Up in London, taking some sort of course. They don't offer formal instruction for the kind of work she's best suited for, though she's had enough experience that she doesn't need any further tutelage." Alsatia, though barely twenty-one, had earned a reputation for being no better than she should be, having an affinity for chauffeurs, under-gardeners, and grooms who were ill-bred, rough around the edges, and sexually attractive.

There seemed to be no polite rejoinder to that. There was little love lost between the siblings, who barely tolerated each other at the best of times.

Before I could attempt to change the subject, Giles was off on a rant about his sister and the money she cost the family with her various scrapes. As I listened, waiting for an opportune moment to inject a change of subject, I began to feel deuced odd. I could hear Giles speaking, as if from a distance, but the beat of his heart and the throb of the blood in his veins grew ever stronger, until that was all I could hear. At that point, all I could think about was how desperately I needed to be able to get up from my chair and take Giles in my arms. I wanted to bite his handsome neck more than I had ever wanted anything.

"Simon. Simon!" Giles spoke with increasing urgency, and my vision cleared long enough for me to see him standing over me, alarm in his face. "What's wrong? You have the queerest look on your face? Are you ill?"

"Pill," I managed to croak. My right hand fumbled at the inside pocket of my jacket, and Giles, understanding, reached inside and retrieved the pillbox, opened it, and extracted a pill for me. My hand was shaking too badly to manage to get the pill on my own, so I simply opened my mouth, and Giles dropped the pill inside. I swallowed. Giles disappeared for a moment, then came back with a glass of water. He held the glass to my mouth, and I took a few sips.

The pill acted quickly, and in a few moments, my vision had cleared completely and my hands had stopped shaking. The sound of Giles's heartbeat had also receded. He knelt by my side, worry writ large in his face.

"Will you be all right now, Simon? Or should I summon a doctor?"

"No, Giles, thank you, I'll be okay in a moment."

"What happened, Simon? I was afraid for a moment you were going to collapse."

"Sorry to alarm you. Just a very minor heart condition," I said, and in a way it was true. "As long as I take my medication, everything is fine. I must have forgotten to take my pill when I should have." That was a lie. I *had* taken my pill, had even taken an extra one, but this batch must be particularly weak. When I returned to Laurel Cottage, I would order a new supply posthaste.

"If you're sure, Simon," Giles said, seating himself across from me. "But you still look a bit peaked."

The pill I had just taken must have been a full-strength one, for I could feel myself returning to normal. I smiled at him. "I'm really fine, Giles. The pill has done its job, and there's nothing that need worry you."

Giles continued to regard me with concern, and I decided a change of subject was most definitely in order.

"Tell me what you know about Jessamy Cholmondley-Pease, Giles."

"Jessamy?" Giles grinned. "Beyond her obvious lack of taste and breeding, you mean?"

I forbore to comment, and he continued. "She was the first to ring Mummy and offer her services, to assist in any way she could. She seemed utterly fascinated by Harwood, and I'd say she was willing to do anything she could to get close to him." He shrugged. "But I'm afraid she was disappointed in that regard. He wouldn't allow anyone but members of his crew to enter the drawing room. I daresay poor Jessamy got little reward for her labors."

"But she was here yesterday, while Harwood and his crew were at work?"

"Oh, yes," Giles said. "She practically haunted the hallway, getting in the way more often than she did anything of use. She kept trying to talk to Dittany Harwood, of all people, but whenever Zeke spotted her, she would scamper off. Mummy wanted to send her away, but she didn't want to offend the woman because of her husband."

"Ah, yes, dear old Desmond. Your mother wouldn't want to alienate the local councillor, I take it."

Giles shook his head. "Mummy has some project cooking that would need his approval, and she didn't want to risk queering the pitch. Our Jessamy fair rides roughshod over her husband, and he daren't do anything that she was against."

"Interesting," I said. "What else do you know about her? Age, background, and so on."

"I presume you'll explain to me at some point why this great interest in her?" Giles waited for my nod before going on. "She's local, actually. Grew up here, and her father, name of Macleod, was actually head gardener here in my grandfather's time. According to what my father told me, years ago Grandfather and Macleod were great cronies. My grandfather was gardening mad, and he supposedly spent more time with Macleod than he did with my grandmother."

Giles stopped with a laugh. "And if you'd ever known my grandmother, Simon, you'd understand why. She died when I was six or seven, and a more sour, desiccated specimen I've yet to meet. She terrified me."

I found these bits of family history interesting, but I wasn't sure they were much to the point. "And Jessamy?" I prompted him.

"I reckon she's pushing fifty," Giles said, "though if you asked her, she's just turned thirty. She certainly tries to dress that way, though if she convinces anyone, they must be blind."

"Has she always lived in Snupperton Mumsley?"

"No. According to local gossip, she was no better than she should have been when she was a teenager, and ran off to London with some kind of traveling salesman. She came back about fifteen years ago, no sign of a child or a wedding ring, met dear old Des, and married him. His star began to rise after that, because Jessamy relentlessly pushed him into local politics." He paused. "To give the devil her due, she's rather shrewd and has a good head for politics. Together they make a pretty effective team."

Giles's eyes sparkled with interest. "Now, Simon, why all this interest in Jessamy?"

I told him about finding her lurking in the bushes outside the drawing room last night. "I think it would be a good idea to find out what she was doing there."

"Oh, most definitely," Giles said. "Wouldn't it be absolutely delicious if Jessamy turned out to be the murderer?"

Chapter Sixteen

A knock on the door interrupted further speculation upon Jessamy Cholmondley-Pease's possible guilt in the murder of Zeke Harwood.

"Yes?" Giles called.

Thompson opened the door. "Begging your pardon, Sir Giles," he said, "but you are needed in the library. The detective inspector wishes a word with you."

"Very well, Thompson," Giles said, rising. "I'll be right down."

"Very good, sir," Thompson responded, closing the door.

"Would you like me to hang around, Giles? If not, I think I'll track down Jessamy and try to winkle the truth out of her."

"I think tackling our Jessamy is most definitely in order," Giles said, heading for the door. "But if there's some sort of emergency, I'll ring you on your mobile."

I followed Giles in more leisurely fashion downstairs. I had thought I might encounter Lady Prunella again and be needed in my new role as advisor and comforter to her ladyship, but evidently she was seeking solace elsewhere at the moment. No one else sought to detain me, and I was soon in my car, heading in search of our Jessamy.

The Cholmondley-Peases lived on the other side of Snupperton Mumsley from Blitherington Hall, on a small but upscale estate not far from my own Laurel Cottage. The estate consisted of five very posh mock-Tudor houses, each every bit as pretentious as the other. Four of them, according to what I had been told, were weekend "cottages" belonging to businessmen who lived and worked in London during the week and who retreated to Snupperton Mumsley for a taste of village life.

On the brief drive I reviewed and discarded several approaches for getting the desired information out of Jessamy, finally settling upon the one I suspected would appeal most to her vanity.

I parked in front of the house and walked up the path to the door. Before I had the chance to knock, the door opened to reveal a smiling Violet Glubb.

"Fancy meeting you here, Mr. Kayjay," she gushed. "You come to call on Mrs. Ceepee?"

"Hello, Vi," I said, stepping into the hallway. "Fancy meeting *you* here." I peeled off my hat and gloves and handed them to the daily, who stood there looking at them with a frown. Finally she plunked them down on a nearby table and turned back to beam cheerfully at me. "Mrs. Ceepee's back in the kitchen, if you'll just come along. She sent me to the door because she was busy chin-wagging on the phone."

"How long have you been working for Mrs., um, Ceepee?" I asked, rather doubting that Jessamy would relish her chatting on the phone being described as "chin-wagging."

"Since last week," Vi said, leading me down the hallway. "She has terrible trouble, she says, keeping help, what with her and her hubby entertaining so much. There's ever so much cleaning to do, but I told her, Vi Glubb has never backed off from a challenge, and what's a few extra dirty dishes, I says."

Vi kept me entertained in such fashion all the way to the kitchen, and I had little time to notice much about the decor of the hallway, other than that it was quite tasteful. Someone besides Jessamy must have been in charge of that, I speculated rather cattily. I had frankly been surprised not to find the walls covered in some sort of dreadful leopard-print wallpaper.

Vi thrust open the door to the kitchen and announced, "It's Mr. Kirby-Jones from Laurel Cottage, mum, come to call. You want I should put the kettle on for tea?"

A telephone stuck in her ear, Jessamy looked up with a frown, quickly masked. "Yes, next Tuesday at eight. Yes, that's fine. Ta very much." She put down the receiver, then stood up. "This is an unexpected pleasure, Professor."

But not a very welcome one, I could tell from her body language. Jessamy was stuck, however, with Vi watching us both avidly. She couldn't ask me to leave, because no doubt she feared Vi would soon have it all over the village how rude she had been to that nice American bloke from Laurel Cottage. I hid a smile, grateful after all for Vi's presence.

"I beg your pardon for calling upon you in such a cavalier fashion, dear lady," I said in my smoothest tones. "I know you keep quite busy, but I did hope you might spare me a few minutes of your time."

"Certainly, Professor," Jessamy said. She turned to her daily, who had a hand hovering over the teakettle. "Yes, Vi, I do think a spot of tea would be lovely. I think we'll go to the sun room, and you may serve us there."

She strode out of the room from a door near the table where she had been working, and I followed while Vi busied herself making the tea.

We stepped through what looked like a mud room, re-plete with old shoes, boots, and other odds and ends, into a chamber that no doubt had been advertised as a sun room. The outside wall was lined floor to ceiling with thick glass panes, looking out upon a small garden. The archi-tect had neglected one important factor, however: this room was on the south side of the house, so it would catch neither the morning nor the evening sun. That was just fine with me, because having to talk with Jessamy while I wore a hat, gloves, and sunglasses would have appeared most peculiar.

"What a lovely room," I said, and I meant it. Despite the lack of sun, the chamber was comfortable and, more-over, tastefully appointed. What a conundrum. Looking at Jessamy, as usual attired in her signature fabric and sport-ing outrageously fluffy, high-heeled mules, I couldn't get the decor to jibe with her own taste in clothing. That was not my concern at the moment, though, and I forced my-self to focus on the task at hand.

"Thank you, Professor," Jessamy said. "Won't you sit down?" She indicated a chair across from where she perched on an overstuffed sofa.

"I'll be quite candid," I lied, "and won't beat around the bush with you, Mrs. Cholmondley-Pease. I need the help of someone who has her finger on the pulse of the vil-lage, so to speak, and naturally I thought of you."

That flattery did its work, I could see. "You don't need to be so formal with me, Professor," she said, beaming. "Do call me Jessamy."

"And I'm Simon." I smiled back at her.

"Now what can I do for you?"

"Well, no doubt you already know that I'm a writer?"

She nodded. "History books, or something like that. I'm not much for history, I'm afraid, unless it's a love story." She giggled. "If you ever write one of them, let me know."

I smiled politely. I couldn't tell her outright that I wrote historical romances under the name of Dorinda Darlington, because I preferred to keep that under wraps. Perhaps I could hint, though. I leaned forward, as if about to confide in her. "Actually, Jessamy, I *do* write other things, things that I am persuaded you would enjoy, but my publisher prefers that I keep my identity a secret. You understand, I'm sure."

She appeared a bit confused at first, but then she nodded. A knowing look passed across her face. "Got you, Simon. Your secret's safe with me."

In a pig's eye, I thought. It would be all over the village by this afternoon that I probably wrote erotica. Oh, well.

"Thank you, Jessamy. Now, this is what I need your help with. I want to write a true crime book about this latest murder in our village. Since the victim is someone so prominent, I think it's bound to be a best-seller, don't you?"

Eyes widening in alarm, Jessamy shrank back against the sofa. "I don't know if that's such a good idea, Simon."

"I know it might seem quite shocking at first, Jessamy, but think of it this way. Someone else is bound to write about it if I don't, and that someone will be from outside the village. Someone who doesn't have a clue about who the really important people in the village are. Someone who might easily misinterpret things people have said and done."

She considered that for a moment. "That's a very good point. It wouldn't do to have someone make us all look bad, would it?"

"Most assuredly not," I said, fervently sincere. "We *must* protect our good names, don't you think?"

"Oh yes," she said, her head bobbing up and down with great emphasis.

"I have already been speaking with Sir Giles and Lady Prunella Blitherington," I went on. "They have assured me of *their* fullest cooperation in my project, because they understand the value of having one of their own take charge of it." I had slightly underlined the words "one of their own," and Jessamy's eyes gleamed at the thought of being included in the same group with the village's first family. "Just as I am quite certain *you* do."

I really should be ashamed of myself, I sometimes thought. But I usually wasn't.

"Now, you understand I must ask quite a lot of questions in order to get as much background as possible?"

"Oh, certainly," Jessamy said. She was so caught up in the idea that she didn't even ask me why I wasn't taking notes, nor did she seem overly concerned that I would ask her about our little encounter in the bushes outside Blitherington Hall last night. She could of course already have prepared her story.

Before I could continue, Vi came in with the tea tray and plunked it down on a table near Jessamy. "You want I should play mother, mum?"

Suppressing a pained look, Jessamy said, "Thank you, Vi, but that won't be necessary. I don't want to keep you from your work."

That was certainly pointed enough, but Vi seemed to take no offense. With a little wave, she departed for the kitchen.

"The woman really is a treasure, Simon," Jessamy said, as she bent over the tea tray, "but she is the tiniest bit encroaching, don't you think?"

Aware that Vi even now was probably standing with her ear to the door, I replied, "Oh, she is certainly a treasure, Jessamy. I've been quite pleased with her work thus far."

Fortunately, Jessamy did not take that for a snub. "How do you take your tea, Simon?"

"A dash of milk and no sugar, please," I said, knowing that if I managed three sips, I would have had plenty.

I accepted the proffered tea and settled back to begin my questioning.

"I don't know whether you've read many mystery novels, Jessamy, but I rather adore them," I said. "I quite fancy myself as Hercule Poirot, exercising the 'leetle grey cells,' as he always says."

Jessamy tittered. "I read one or two of them, but they're ever so much better on the telly, don't you think, Simon?"

"Yes, they are delightful, aren't they? Well, you see, Jessamy, if I'm going to write this book, I have to gather evidence the way Poirot does. In my case, of course, the police aren't going to ask me to consult with them, so I have to do it on my own."

She was listening with fierce concentration, nodding as I babbled along.

"Giles did tell me how helpful you had been, assisting at Blitherington Hall, and of course the fact that you were there and no doubt might have seen *something* of significance is extremely helpful. I imagine that you're quite an *observant* sort of person, aren't you?"

I could feel the unease and the doubt beginning to stir. She was torn between wanting to be known as an observant person and not wanting to be questioned too closely about that little episode in the bushes. Softly, softly, catchee monkey, as the old saying went.

"I do notice things, Simon, things that often slip by other people," she said with caution. "Naturally, with such a celebrity in the village, I wanted to do my part to help Snupperton Mumsley put its best foot forward. I do have a certain position to uphold."

"Naturally," I said, echoing her. "Now, Jessamy, I want you to think back to yesterday. Did you notice anything out of the ordinary? Or did you happen to hear anything at all odd?"

Jessamy's eyes grew round with excitement. "Now that

I come to think of it, Simon, I did hear something that could turn out to be *very* important."

"And what did you hear?" I asked with what I thought was commendable patience when the pause went on a bit too long.

"I heard that dishy director say, 'I'm warning you, Zeke, I'll make you pay for this!' "

Chapter Seventeen

That did sound promising, and she wasn't lying. I had feared she might make something up to deflect my attention, but I felt she was telling me the truth.

"That is most interesting, Jessamy," I said approvingly. "Tell me more. When and where did you happen to overhear this?"

She beamed like a child who had just earned a gold star from her teacher. "Happen I was passing by the billiard room, Simon, and I heard loud voices." She wrinkled her nose. "Lady Prunella had told everyone that if they must smoke inside Blitherington Hall, then they were allowed to do so in the billiard room. I don't think she meant them to leave the door open, because as I happened by, the hallway was simply reeking of smoke."

Lady Prunella was well known in the village as an anti-smoking crusader. Her late husband, a man addicted to his cigars and pipes, had died of lung cancer.

"I thought I had better close the door," Jessamy said, "because someone was smoking a cigar, and we all know how Lady P. feels about that!"

I nodded.

With a girlish laugh she continued, "Well, naturally, I couldn't resist the tiniest peek inside, and there was that very handsome director puffing away on a big cigar, and poor Mr. Harwood was smoking a cigarette." She paused for dramatic emphasis. "And that was when I heard Mr. Weatherstone threaten him!"

"Did you see what happened?"

"Oh, my, yes," she said. "Mr. Weatherstone was looming over Mr. Harwood and waving his cigar in a threatening manner. Mr. Harwood took a step back and said, 'Don't be such a tired drama queen, Cliffie darling. You're simply not up to the American job, and that's all there is to it. Be grateful you've ridden my coattails for this long.' "

"My, my," I said. "That was rather rude."

Jessamy's eyes grew rounder. "Oh yes, and I thought Mr. Weatherstone was going to stick his cigar right in Mr. Harwood's face after that. If you could only have seen the look on his face! I'm surprised he didn't kill him right then and there."

"What happened next?"

She colored slightly. "I must have made a sound of distress, because they both turned and saw me at the door."

"That was unfortunate," I said.

"They both glared at me in the most unfriendly manner," Jessamy complained. "So I mumbled something at them about the smoke getting out into the hall and Lady P. being upset and pulled the door shut. I got away from that door as fast as I could, let me tell you!"

"Did you hear anything further?"

"No. Not long after, I had to leave the Hall to take care of some errands in the village."

"Have you informed Detective Inspector Chase about this yet?"

"No," she said, and I could hear the disappointment in her voice. "I've not had the opportunity yet."

"I'm sure you'll be able to talk to him soon," I said. Now to go in for the kill, so to speak. "You did, of course, return to the Hall later that evening, didn't you?"

She stiffened. "Well, yes, I did." She wasn't going to volunteer anything.

"When I saw you," I said, trying to phrase it diplomatically, "you were outside, near the French windows."

"Oh yes," she said. "I had almost forgotten about that." Her laugh failed to convince me that her errand had been innocuous. "Silly me. I'm forever losing things, and I had been out there at some point in the afternoon. I discovered that I had dropped an earring, and as it was one of a most expensive pair that Des had given me for our last anniversary, I simply *had* to find it. Des would have been livid. He's always nattering on at me about losing things."

She was lying to me. I could tell by the change in her breathing and her heart rate. If her earring had been somewhere in the bushes near the French windows, I suspected it was because she had deliberately dropped it there so she would have an excuse to come back later and nose around.

I pretended to accept her story. "How long had you been searching for it when I encountered you?"

"Oh, just a few minutes," she said carelessly. "Lucky for me, I found it almost straightaway."

"That means you must have arrived after the police?"

That caught her up. "Er, yes, I suppose so."

That was too obvious a lie. She must have been there for quite some time. It's a wonder the police didn't spot her, but she must have hidden herself rather well. I hadn't spotted her car anywhere, and if she had truly been on such an innocent errand, she would not have hesitated to park in the forecourt of the Hall. Her story didn't add up.

"Then that also means that you didn't observe anything of what went on in the drawing room?"

"Heavens, no," she said, protesting a bit too loudly. She

had seen something, I was sure, but what? And how would I convince her to confide in me? Had she seen the killer? Surely she wasn't going to attempt a spot of black-mail; she would only find herself in a dangerous situation if she did.

Someone coughed behind me, and both Jessamy and I started. We turned to see Vi standing there.

"Begging your pardon, I'm sure, mum," she said, "but the police is here. You want I should show them in here?"

I stood up quickly. "I had best be going along, Jessamy," I said. "But I shall want to talk to you again. I feel certain there is so much you can tell me to help me with my project."

She caught the meaning in my words, and her face flushed slightly. "That's as may be," she replied. "Yes, Vi, you can show the police in here."

I inclined my head in her direction, and she averted her eyes, unable to look me in the face. I bade Vi good day and preceded her from the room. Near the front door Robin Chase and Sergeant Harper stood waiting. A pained expression crossed Robin's face as he realized who Jessamy's visitor had been.

"Already hard at work on the case, I see, Simon," he said. "Or should I say, Miss Marple?"

"So *very* amusing, Robin," I said as I picked up my hat and gloves from the table where Vi had placed them. "I can't see why you should object to my paying social calls upon my neighbors."

"If I thought you were merely paying a social call, I shouldn't object in the least," Robin observed mildly. "But I fear I know you better than that, Simon." The corners of his mouth twitched.

I forbore to respond to that as I pulled on my gloves and placed my hat on my head. "Good day, Robin, Sergeant." I moved past them to the door.

"Ah, Simon," Robin said, halting me. "If you will be at home in the next little while, I would like to talk to you."

"Certainly, Robin," I said, turning back for a moment. "My door is always open to you."

One hand reached up to stroke his moustache. He always did that when he was nervous or disconcerted. I seemed to have that effect on him, quite regularly. I suppressed a smile. "I shall look forward to your visit, then."

With that parting shot, I departed. Minutes later, I was back home. I went upstairs to change into my working togs, and once back downstairs in my office, I thought I had better do something about a fresh supply of my pills before I got lost in work.

I called the number in London and spoke to one of the staff, who offered profuse apologies when I explained my problem. He promised to see that I received a fresh supply as soon as possible, and I thanked him.

That task out of the way, I booted up the computer and sat staring at the screen. Instead of focusing on the work at hand, however, I found my mind wandering instead over the details of the murder of Zeke Harwood.

There were a number of interesting possibilities. The existence of a secret entrance to the drawing room presented certain difficulties. If the crime scene staff found no evidence that anyone other than Lady Prunella had made use of the secret stairway, then Lady Prunella's position was invidious indeed. Her motive for killing Harwood seemed rather ridiculous, but unless the police were unable to uncover anything stronger, Lady Prunella might find herself in considerable hot water.

If, on the other hand, they found evidence that someone else had made use of it, that would take some of the pressure off Lady P. For the sake of Giles and his mother, I sincerely hoped that such evidence would indeed be found.

The secret stairway could be nothing more than a red herring, however. Zeke Harwood might have discovered its existence, but that didn't mean he had told anyone else about it, or that anyone else had discovered it by accident. In that case, we were back to the locked room puzzle that wasn't much of a locked room puzzle. Given that several people had laid hands on the victim once we were inside the drawing room, it would have been very easy for the murderer to slip the key to the drawing room back into Harwood's pocket. The question, of course, was who?

Perhaps the police would turn up some evidence of that. In the haste of the moment, the killer might have been a bit careless and have left a fingerprint on the key. I rather doubted that, however, because this whole case smacked of cool deliberation. The way I read the situation, the killer had seized an opportunity and acted ruthlessly and quickly. That meant someone who could think and act fast.

Which brought me right back again to *who?* Who had the most compelling motive? And who had the necessary coolness of thought and deed? I hadn't spent enough time with the main suspects to be able to decide. I examined each of my main suspects in turn: Piers Limpley, Dittany Harwood, Moira Rhys-Morgan, and Cliff Weatherstone. None of them had impressed me thus far as having the qualities I deemed necessary.

I could easily see where they might all have motives for getting rid of Harwood, with the possible exception of Moira Rhys-Morgan. She was the only one of the group who seemed genuinely to mourn the man. He had been rather unpleasant and hadn't treated his associates very well, but the motive for his death had to lie in something deeper than ill treatment.

Unless the worm had turned. In that case, I could easily

see Cliff Weatherstone or Piers Limpley in the role of murderer. In fact, I rather favored Cliffie as the murderer, but that might have been mere prejudice on my part.

A knock on my front door interrupted further reflections. I supposed Robin had come to call, and I glanced down at my working togs. They were a bit on the ratty side, because I like old and comfortable clothes when I'm writing. I should have thought of that while I was changing, but my mind had been occupied by other matters. Robin had seen me like this before, however, so I supposed it didn't matter.

I went to the front door and opened it. To my surprise, it was not Robin Chase and his sergeant who stood there. Cliff Weatherstone had come to call.

"This is indeed an unexpected pleasure," I said coolly, standing back to allow Weatherstone to enter. He clumped past me into the hall and turned back to face me once I had closed the door.

His face flushed in annoyance, Cliff faced me defiantly. "Trust me, Professor, I wouldn't be here if the situation weren't desperate."

"Indeed," I said, observing him. He was upset by something. One hand fiddled with something in his pocket, and his whole demeanor bespoke worry. "And you're here to see me because you think I can do something about it? How too, too flattering."

He took a deep breath. "You don't have to be insulting. I know you don't like me, but I can't help it if you're jealous. I wouldn't be here if Giles hadn't insisted I talk to you."

"This was Giles's idea, then?" I said.

Cliff scowled. "He seems to think you hung the sun and the stars, *why* I cannot imagine. But he says you have experience with this kind of thing."

"What kind of thing?" I said, deliberately refusing to help, though I figured I knew perfectly well what he meant.

"Murders," he said, fairly spitting out the word. "According to Giles, dead bodies seem to keep popping up all over the place whenever you're around. He says you've been quite successful in solving murders before."

"Giles is much too kind," I said, but Cliff ignored the irony.

"You've got to help me," Cliff said. "If you don't, they'll arrest me for a murder I didn't commit!"

Chapter Eighteen

"My, my," I said, allowing my amusement to show. "You *are* in rather a state, aren't you?"

Cliff emitted a sound of disgust and started to thrust past me. "I should have known you'd respond like this. Just forget I ever came here, will you?"

I placed a restraining hand on his arm, and he paused, taken aback by the strength of my grip. "Do calm yourself, Cliff," I drawled. "I didn't say I wouldn't help you."

Rubbing his arm, he glared at me. "You've a funny way of helping."

"Come into the sitting room, and tell me all about it," I said, marching into said room and seating myself in the most comfortable chair. He followed me and sat in the chair to which I directed him. It was not a very comfortable chair, but I didn't mind if he squirmed a bit—physically or mentally.

"There's a humidor on the table," I said. "I indulge in the occasional cigar. Help yourself if you feel in need of a smoke."

Almost as a reflex he leaned forward and stretched a hand toward the humidor. Then he drew sharply back.

"How do you know I'm a cigar smoker? You've never seen me smoke one."

I waited, smiling, while he thought it over. "I suppose you might have sniffed me out," he mused. But then a scowl spread over his face as he figured it out. "That bloody Pease woman. She must have told you about the little scene she overheard between Zeke and me."

"Clever Cliff," I said. "Yes, dear Jessamy did confide in me. I must say, I imagine Detective Inspector Chase will take a dim view of a threat like that."

He did not respond to the bait. Instead, he reached for the humidor again, opened it, and took a moment to select a cigar. His choice made, he closed the humidor, then picked up the cigar cutter lying on the table and clipped the end off the cigar. He dropped the end into an ashtray on the table and picked up the lighter.

I watched in amusement as he toasted the end of the cigar, then put the cigar in his mouth to light it. The ritual of preparing and lighting a cigar was a good delaying tactic, and Cliff was taking full advantage of it. Once he had the cigar burning to his satisfaction, he exhaled a long plume of smoke into the air.

"Very nice," he said. "Cubans are the finest, aren't they?"

"One of the advantages of residing in England," I said.

"Yes," Cliff said. "What I said to Zeke, which that interfering cow overheard, *was* a threat, I suppose." He paused for another draw on the cigar. "Sure you won't join me?"

"Not just now, thanks," I said. His agitation had calmed, though I could still sense an undercurrent of unease. "Why were you threatening Harwood?"

I knew the reason, of course, but I couldn't admit to having overheard his conversation with Giles in the pub.

"Zeke had dumped me. Professionally, that is," Cliff said. "He was heading off to the States, and Yours Truly was not invited along, despite the fact that I had been with him from the beginning and knew more about directing him than anyone else ever possibly could."

"A professional insult," I said. "How unfortunate. What kind of repercussions would that have had for your career?"

"A momentary setback, nothing more," Cliff said. "I've turned down a number of good offers because of Zeke, and I would soon have had something else lined up."

"If that's the case," I pointed out, "then why would you need to threaten Harwood? Seems to me you might have been glad to get rid of him and work with someone less unpleasant."

Cliff snorted, smoke billowing out of his mouth. "That person doesn't exist. Zeke was no different from most of the other *talent* I've ever worked with. They all have egos the size of Russia and a vastly inflated idea of their importance to the world."

"I see. What a lovely bunch of folk with whom to associate."

"It pays well," Cliff said.

"So does prostitution, or so I've heard," I said.

Cliff half-rose from his chair, thought better of it, and subsided without saying anything.

He had more self-control than I had imagined; I'd have to credit him that.

"I fail to see the source of your agitation," I said. "If your threat was an empty one, then why the panic? Why are you so worried that the police will consider you Suspect Number One?"

"Because," Cliff said, contemplating the ash on his cigar, "someone is bound to tell them that I once knocked Zeke flat on his fat, lying arse." He leaned over and tapped the ash into the ashtray.

"My, you do have a temper, don't you?" I said. "When and why did you plant Harwood such a facer?"

Cliff smiled in satisfaction. "The bastard had it coming to him. It was about two years ago, I reckon. Until then, he wouldn't keep his hands off me. Always pawing me, whenever anyone else was around, making suggestive remarks to the effect that he and I were having a torrid affair. He even had the cheek once to tell someone the reason he kept me on was because of my skill between the sheets."

"Rather than your abilities as a producer and director?" I really did try not to sound skeptical, but Cliff flushed anyway.

"Considering that Zeke was about as physically appealing as what the cat coughed up, no, I didn't fancy him, not in the least."

"I can't argue with that," I said.

Cliff smiled, then dropped his bombshell. "Moreover, Zeke was about as gay as Maggie Thatcher. It was all an act." He sat back, drew on his cigar, and awaited my reaction.

For once, I was momentarily speechless. I shook my head, as if to clear it.

"That fairly boggles the mind," I said at last. "Why on earth would he pretend to be gay?"

Cliff laughed. "Because he thought that was what everyone expected of someone who was an interior designer. And because he got more press out of it. He could be as flamboyant as he liked, and no one thought anything of it. Because he was a flashy queen, you see."

"I do see," I said. "It makes an absurd kind of sense. And I must admit that he had me completely fooled."

"Our Zeke was a good actor," Cliff said. "I'll grant him that. He might have had a fair career on the stage, but he genuinely loved what he did."

"And became enormously successful at it," I said. "Which means much would have been at stake if someone had got wind of the truth."

"I suppose," Cliff said. "Zeke preferred his image to stay as he had constructed it, but I'm not so certain that his public wouldn't have forgiven him, pretty quickly, even if the truth had gotten out."

"Was that what you were threatening him with? Telling the press that he wasn't gay and had been shamming all this time?"

Cliff nodded. "I thought it might at least make him think twice about dropping me the way he had planned."

"Did it?" I asked. "Make him think twice?"

"He said he would think it over," Cliff replied. "And I've no idea now what he might have decided, because someone killed him before he could tell me. And that someone was not I."

I was halfway inclined to believe him. Though I didn't much care for Cliff, I had to admit that he didn't seem stupid enough to have killed Harwood over losing his job. Perhaps the lure of television success in the States was stronger than his intellect. That seemed unlikely, however, because by killing Harwood, Cliff would have definitely lost, while as long as Harwood was alive, there was the chance he might reconsider and keep Cliff on as a member of his staff.

"Well, then," I said, "if *you* didn't kill Harwood, who did? It had to have been someone who knew him."

"That's where you come in, according to Giles," Cliff said, smoke coming from his mouth in small bursts as he spoke. "He seems to think you'll figure it out all much faster than the copper."

"However flattered I might be by Giles's faith in me," I said, "I can't just barge in and start questioning people.

Detective Inspector Chase would be quite annoyed, for one thing."

"Again according to Giles," Cliff said, "that's never stopped you before." He smiled smugly around the cigar in his mouth.

I decided to ignore that. "If I were to manage somehow to question the other suspects," I said, placing slight emphasis on the word *other,* "without riling Detective Inspector Chase, where should I start? What can you tell me that would be helpful?"

Cliff drew angrily on his cigar. "You might find that the *other* suspects had stronger reasons to be shed of Zeke than I did, Simon. You might start with Moira Rhys-Morgan. Zeke has treated her like dirt for years."

"Oh, how so?"

"The bloody woman's been in love with him for years, though I haven't the slightest idea *why*. Zeke knew it, and he manipulated her like a marionette. He hopped in and out of her bed when it suited him, and she just let him do it. But maybe she finally got tired of being treated so badly."

"That motive I could believe," I said, "if what you say is true."

"You don't have to take my word for it," Cliff said. "You can see she's the only one of us who's grieving for the bastard. That much should be obvious, even to you."

I refused to be ruffled by the venom in his tone. "So much for Mrs. Rhys-Morgan. Who else?"

Cliff shrugged. "Poor Piers has been carrying a torch for Moira for years. But she wouldn't look at him as long as Zeke was in the picture. Maybe he did it in a fit of jealous rage? He hated the way Zeke treated Moira."

"Another good motive," I said. Trust a vicious queen to know the real dirt. "And Dittany?"

"There you've got me," Cliff said. "There was little love lost between brother and sister, I can tell you that much. But Dittany was the only one of us who would really stand up to Zeke and make him back down occasionally. Neither one of them would ever talk much about their childhood, though of course Zeke was quite a bit older than Dittany. In fact, Zeke never talked much about his family or the distant past."

"That would certainly bear investigation," I said. "Sounds to me like there was something he wanted kept hidden."

A knock sounded on the front door before Cliff could respond.

"That will be Detective Inspector Chase," I told him, my voice low. "He said he would be coming round to talk to me. It would be better for both of us if he did not find you here. Did you walk here, or drive?"

"I walked," Cliff said, his decibel level matching mine. "Why?"

"Then there's no car outside to give us away," I said. "You can slip out the back door, in the kitchen, and go around the side of the house once he's inside." I stood up. "Come along, better get going."

"If you say so," Cliff responded. He followed me to the hall, and I pointed the way to the kitchen. The knock sounded again as I watched Cliff disappear into the kitchen, but I waited until I heard the back door open and close softly before I opened the front door.

Robin Chase stood there alone. "Good afternoon, Robin," I said, motioning for him to step aside. "And where is the good sergeant?"

"He's gone into the village to buy some cigarettes," Robin said.

"Ah," I said, "so you wanted to speak to me alone." I

leaned against the closed door and regarded him with interest. He was fingering his moustache.

"Well, yes," Robin admitted. "I need your help, unofficially of course, and I didn't want Harper to overhear me."

Chapter Nineteen

I regarded Robin with considerable amusement. "So now I'm to play Miss Marple to your Inspector Craddock? My, my, what will the good citizens of St. Mary Mead think?"

"You must have your little joke, Simon," Robin said. "I quite understand that, after the grief I've given you over your past inter . . . rather, assistance with my investigations."

"Nice save, Robin," I said, walking past him and into the sitting room.

Robin followed me, sniffing inquisitively. "I had no idea you were a cigar smoker, Simon."

I turned a bland face to him. "I daresay there's quite a lot you don't know about me, Robin. There's certainly much about *you* I don't know." I sat down.

Robin wisely avoided the chair earlier vacated by Cliff Weatherstone and instead chose a much more comfortable one. "Yes, well, Simon, that's not why I called upon you just now."

"No, I suppose not." I sighed with deep regret. "Help yourself to one of my cigars if you'd like."

"Don't mind if I do," Robin said. "I don't often indulge, mind you, but the occasional cigar can't hurt you."

I watched as Robin repeated the ritual so recently enacted by Cliff Weatherstone. He was smiling widely by the time he exhaled his first mouthful of smoke. I decided upon impulse to join him, and he waited until I had my own fired up. We then sat and smoked in silence for a moment.

"You were saying, Robin," I finally prodded him, "that you wanted my help."

He tapped ash into the ashtray before responding. "Yes, Simon, I would like your help. But it has to be strictly *sub rosa,* of course."

"Of course, Robin," I said. "I wouldn't like to see you in trouble with your superiors for enlisting my aid."

"Quite," he said, smiling around his cigar. "You do seem to have a certain knack for being johnny-on-the-spot when these things happen, Simon." He held up a hand to forestall the protest he no doubt was expecting. "I'm not saying that you are in any way responsible for the murders that keep happening around you, naturally. But you do seem to be in the right place at the wrong time. Or is it in the wrong place at the right time?"

He laughed at his own little joke while I smoked in silence.

"Whichever. The thing is, Simon, you somehow manage to winkle things out of people that they won't always reveal to someone official, like me."

"And you want me to winkle things out of people, as you call it?"

"More or less," Robin said. "This whole case has given me quite a few headaches. There are a number of contradictions that need sorting out."

"I'll be delighted to do what I can, Robin," I replied. "But I can do so more effectively if I know more about the case. I wouldn't give anything away to the suspects, of course, but I have to know at least some of what you know, if I'm to accomplish anything worthwhile."

"I quite see that," Robin said, "and I'm prepared to tell you as much as I can." He drew on his cigar.

"Very well," I said. "First I must ask you, do you really consider Lady Prunella a suspect?"

Robin laughed. "I can't rule her out completely, Simon, because she definitely had the means and the opportunity."

"But not really the motive."

He shook his head. "Even as dotty as Lady Prunella is, I rather doubt she would have killed Harwood to stop him from airing that bit of film, or for painting her drawing room walls red."

"Exactly," I said. "The woman can be a complete loon sometimes, but she's not a killer. Whoever did this had the brains to plan a swift and efficient murder, and I can't see Lady Prunella having the brains to do it."

"As you say, Simon, exactly," Robin replied. "The problem is, I can't quite figure which one of them *is* smart enough. None of them seem up to the task, frankly."

"Well, let's come back to that," I said. "First, tell me how Harwood died."

Robin blew a couple of smoke rings before he replied. "Thought I might have lost the knack. Well, we have only preliminary postmortem results at the moment, but the police surgeon says it was three or four blows to the head, two of which could have done it." He frowned. "The trouble is, at least two of the blows came from different blunt objects."

"That's strange," I said, smoking thoughtfully for a moment. "The killer bangs Harwood on the head with object number one, decides it's not doing the job well enough, and picks up object number two. Why wouldn't he just hit harder the second time with object number one?"

"That's part of the puzzle, Simon," Robin said. "And so far we've not found anything that we think was used as either of the murder weapons."

"Curiouser and curiouser, as Alice said." I discarded the ash from my cigar. "Moving on from the murder weapon or weapons. What about the secret stairway? Was there any evidence that someone besides Lady Prunella had used it?"

Robin frowned again. "Evidence of a sort, and that's a puzzle in itself. The stairs are quite dusty on the edges, not to mention the odd cobweb here and there. From what both Lady Prunella and Sir Giles told me, no one has used the staircase in years. If only Lady Prunella had been up and down the stairs, we would have expected to find her footprints in the dust."

I hazarded a guess. "But you didn't find her footprints?"

"No," Robin said. "The steps had been swept more or less clean. Except for the outside edges on either side. We found dust there, but nothing else. No fingerprints, no footprints, nothing."

"How did someone sweep the stairs? And when?"

"In answer to your first question, Simon, we did find the answer to that. But the answer provides another puzzle."

"What do you mean?"

"We found a drop cloth stuffed away in a corner of the drawing room, and the edges of it were quite dusty. The same dust, as far as we can tell until further analysis, as the dust on the edges of the stairs in the secret stairway."

"So someone could have dragged this cloth up or down the stairs to erase footprints."

"Yes," Robin said. "Evidently he or she dragged it down the stairs, since it was left in the drawing room, rather than in the bedroom above."

"Mightn't your technical people be able to tell that by examining the steps more closely?"

"Yes," Robin said. "They're working on that now, but we won't have an answer for a while yet."

"That's definitely an odd twist," I said. I drew in smoke and expelled it as I thought. "Since the drop cloth was left in the drawing room, it might mean the murderer left the room by either the French windows or the drawing room door. Most likely the latter." I repeated my theory as to how the murderer could have placed the key in Harwood's pocket when we found the body.

"As the French windows were locked from the inside and cannot be opened from the outside, even with a key, then it means, if you're correct, that the murderer went out the drawing room door."

"Having gained entrance to the drawing room from the secret stairway, rather than having been admitted by Harwood?"

Robin nodded. "We think Harwood must have been caught by surprise, because there was no evidence anywhere that he struggled with his attacker." He drew on his cigar. "On the other hand, there's no reason to think that he would have expected someone he knew to be planning to murder him, and he could have turned his back on the killer after letting him or her into the room." He leaned forward to tap an inch or so of ash into the ashtray.

"' 'Tis a puzzlement,' as the King of Siam once said," I smiled as I quoted from *The King and I*.

"Unfortunately," Robin said, smiling wryly.

"What about the time of death?" I asked.

"He can't have been dead very long when you found him," Robin said. "The time frame is rather tight, I'm afraid. If Lady Prunella is correct about the time at which she last saw Harwood alive, it doesn't leave much time for someone to have killed him before you all gathered in the library."

I considered that for a moment. It was a matter of fifteen minutes, more or less. I repeated this aloud.

"Yes," Robin said. "Perhaps a quarter of an hour."

"If," I said, placing emphasis on the word, "the killer was one of the people gathered in the library before dinner."

Robin nodded. "And we can't rule out the fact that someone else could have gotten into the drawing room from the bedroom above and killed him while you were all waiting for him in the library from approximately eight o'clock until eight-thirty."

"Except for the fact that the drop cloth that was used to sweep the stairs was found *in* the drawing room. But I suppose the killer could have gone back up the stairs without leaving any real traces."

"Maybe," Robin said, "but the wood of those stairs is old and quite soft in places. The killer might have left some trace. If so, the boffins will find it."

"About those fifteen minutes," I said. "I'm sure you've questioned Limpley, Weatherstone, and the two women about that."

"Of course," Robin replied. "But I got little help there. They all seem to have alibis, oddly enough."

"How so?" I asked.

Robin exhaled smoke. "I think I'll leave it to you to ask them, Simon. For my own reasons, I'd rather that you hear it from them first. I want to get your impressions of what they all told me, and see what you make of it without my prejudicing you in any way." He grinned.

"Odious man," I said. "Now you know you've got my curiosity up, and I'll be beside myself until I talk to them."

"Nothing better than a bloodhound eager for the scent. You get more results that way." Robin stood up. "I had best be going, Simon. Harper will have his cigarettes by now and be wondering where I am."

"And how will you explain where you got the cigar?" I asked.

"Good point," Robin said, looking regretfully at his half-smoked stogie. "Guess I had better jettison the rest of it, though it's a crime to waste such a good cigar."

"You could always tell him you had it with you," I said, standing up to show him to the door.

"Why not?" Robin said, sticking the cigar back in his mouth. "I take it you'll be going over to Blitherington Hall soon, Simon?"

"As soon as I can change my clothes," I said. "Giles is rather expecting me by now, I should think."

"No doubt," Robin said, his face twisting into the semblance of a frown.

Oh, my, I thought, is the handsome detective just the tiniest bit jealous? What an interesting notion.

I opened the door for Robin. "Out you go, Robin. The sooner you're on your way, the sooner I can put Operation Miss Marple into effect. But first I must find where I left my bag of knitting."

Laughing, Robin strode down the walk to the lane and let himself out of the gate. I watched for a moment, blowing smoke into the darkening sky.

Then I went back inside to get dressed. For once I had official, or rather, *semi*-official sanction for my meddling.

Chapter Twenty

I had rather a rude surprise when I walked out the front door of Laurel Cottage. When I had come downstairs again after changing my clothes, I had been vaguely aware of sounds coming from the lane but had paid little attention to them. By now it was early evening, and I had put it down to the noise generated by the usual comings and goings of my fellow villagers at this time of day.

Instead, the noise came from several reporters and television crews camped in the lane outside Laurel Cottage. As I stopped just outside the door, I felt harsh light focus on me as the television cameras drew a bead on me.

I could have ducked back inside, but I wasn't going to cower at home when I was needed at Blitherington Hall. Voices rose and clamored for my attention, questions being shot at me rapid-fire. Slipping on my dark glasses, which considerably toned down the glare, I scanned the group and chose the best-looking male reporter of the group. "You, there. What do you want?"

Smirking at his colleagues, the young man stepped forward. "Just a bit o' your time, Professor," he said, in tones desperately trying not to sound too Cockney. "According to my sources, you've been involved in several murders. Who do you think killed Zeke Harwood?"

This was a facer, no doubt about it. In the past, Robin Chase had kept my involvement in his investigations quiet, and I had not gained the kind of notoriety I sought to avoid. Now, it seemed, the secret was out. I sighed.

Who had leaked my name to the press? And who had told them I had been involved in previous murder investigations? Giles wouldn't have done it, I was sure, nor would Trevor Chase or his cousin, the dashing detective inspector. Lady Prunella might have let it slip, if she had somehow come into contact with the press. But Giles would have done his best to keep his mother away from them, and knowing Lady Prunella as I did, I doubted she had sought them out herself.

No use speculating about it at the moment. I had better make the best of this and be done with it.

"What I think about the murder," I said in my best orotund manner, "is of no consequence, young man. I am *not* a detective, and I have no wish to interfere in the official investigation. Whoever informed you otherwise has misled you dreadfully, I'm afraid."

"Come on, Professor," another reporter called out, "you really can't expect us to believe that. What about the murder of the postmistress a few months ago? Weren't you heavily involved in that?"

Drat and double drat! They were even better informed than I had anticipated. Someone had done a good job of ratting me out, as they say.

Nothing for it, then, but to brazen it out.

"As I have already stated, you have been grossly misinformed. This is, no doubt, someone's idea of a rather distasteful joke. Now, if you will excuse me, I have an engagement for dinner."

Ignoring the calls for my attention, not to mention a few

comments bordering on insults, I stalked around the house to the garage. Backing the Jag out carefully, I drove a little closer to some of the press than they thought comfortable, and they jumped out of my way. One foolish cameraman thought to stop me by standing in the middle of the lane, but I gunned the engine and the Jag jumped forward.

The cameraman jumped backwards, and I roared down the lane a hundred yards or so in the direction of Blitherington Hall. In my wake the press scrambled to follow.

Another contingent of reporters lined the drive to the Hall, but I maneuvered the Jag carefully through them and was soon safely within the portals, away from the attentions of the press.

"Good evening, Thompson," I said. "The press are being rather a nuisance this evening. Do you know, have they spoken with anyone here?"

"Not to my knowledge, Professor," he said, having closed the door behind me. "Sir Giles has been most particular about that. No one has set foot outside the Hall in the past day except for Sir Giles himself and Mr. Weatherstone. Of course, some of the staff have come and gone, as they don't live in, but Sir Giles warned them most particular about talking with reporters. They're a good group, Professor, and I'm sure they wouldn't have carried tales to the press."

Thompson had turned quite loquacious with me of late, no doubt a sign of the thawing of relations between his mistress and me. "Thank you, Thompson. The less we have to do with the press for now, the better. Now, where might I find Sir Giles?"

Thompson directed me to the library. With the police for the moment not occupying the room, Giles was ensconced there, beavering away at something.

As I walked down the hallway toward the library, I considered momentarily that Cliff Weatherstone might have been the one to bear tales to the press, but I quickly dismissed the thought. He might have heard about the earlier murders from Giles, but I could see nothing he had to gain from embroiling me with the press. I suspected that someone who had a grudge against me had been behind that distasteful episode.

Giles was frowning over a sheaf of papers clinched in his hands when I entered the library. He set them down with a strained smile when he saw me. "Good evening, Simon. I'm pleased you're here. The atmosphere in this house is abominably strained, and I shall be thankful when we can see the last of these so-called guests of ours."

I suppressed the urge to ask whether he included Cliff Weatherstone in that group.

"Evening, Giles," I said. "I'll do my best to help you rid yourself of all of them as quickly as possible." I sat down in one of the chairs before the desk.

"What is that you're frowning over so?"

Giles scowled. "The bloody contract. With Harwood dead and the work uncompleted, there's the most awful mess in the drawing room. I was reading through the contract to discern whether we could hold Harwood's production company responsible for any repairs, or at least for completing the job."

"Any luck?"

Giles shook his head. "There's no contingency for the death of the decorator, I'm afraid. Perhaps it's for the best. Once they've all cleared out, we can get on with salvaging what we can. I wish Mummy had never written that bally letter in the first place!"

"Then we need to get this settled as quickly as we can. But first, I must tell you what has just occurred." I gave him a brief report of the scene at Laurel Cottage. He groaned.

"It's bad enough that we have the press practically

camped outside the Hall, but that you should have to be subjected to the same treatment is intolerable, Simon."

"Thank you, dear boy," I said soothingly, "but don't fret yourself. I didn't tell you about it to distress you. It will be sorted out, and when I discover the identity of the person who informed the press, I shall extract a suitable revenge."

Glimpsing the expression on my face, Giles whistled. "I wouldn't want to be that person when you do, Simon."

"Yes, well, down to business then. I presume Cliff Weatherstone told you about his little visit with me?" I waited for Giles's nod, then continued. "I also had a visit from Robin Chase, who enlisted my aid, much to my surprise." I smiled. "I rather believe I'm beginning to wear him down."

"Spare me the details, if you please, Simon, of your campaign to snare the copper." Giles turned away from me to stare moodily at the wall. "If I had realized playing hard to get was the way to proceed, I shouldn't have annoyed you with my attentions."

This jealousy that Giles harbored because of my curiosity over Robin Chase was beginning to get out of hand. "Giles, look at me. Don't be childish. Look at me."

Slowly he obeyed, turning back to face me, and I examined him carefully. I had to proceed with caution, for much was at stake here, perhaps more than I was willing to admit.

"I won't deny that I find Robin attractive. He is physically appealing, and he is something of an enigma, because I can't quite read him. Usually I find men much more transparent. Call it idle curiosity, if you will, but it is really no more than that, Giles. I have no plans to 'snare the copper,' to use your phrase."

"When you look at me like that, Simon," Giles said softly, "I almost begin to believe you."

"You should believe me, Giles," I said. "I wouldn't lie to you, and certainly not about something like this." I might have to omit the truth about my true nature, at least for a while longer, but I wouldn't lie to him about my feelings. "Were I ready to become involved with anyone, it would be you. But you must be patient with me until the time is right."

He sat quietly for the moment and observed me. I tried to probe his emotions, but for once he was playing it very cool, and I couldn't read him. Then, as I watched, he stood up and walked around the desk. Leaning over, he kissed me.

"Fair enough, Simon," Giles said, smiling demurely when he drew away from me. "But I thought you should have some incentive for making up your mind."

"Yes, well, I shall bear that in mind, Giles." I tried to frown at him but I couldn't force my mouth into the correct shape. I was smiling too broadly.

"Back to the other matter at hand," Giles said, seating himself once more behind the desk. "This murder. Before we became sidetracked, you mentioned that the detective inspector had asked for your help."

"Yes," I said, "and he was quite forthcoming about what he and his team know thus far." I stopped, frowning. "I'm afraid I can't share everything he told me, Giles, because he didn't give me leave to discuss it with anyone. Though I must say, I don't believe he considers either you or your mother credible suspects."

"I understand," Giles said, taking it better than I had thought he would.

"One thing I believe I can tell you, however," I said, "is that three of the suspects seem to have an alibi for the time of the murder. Robin wouldn't tell me what it was, saying that he wanted me to hear it from them myself, without his prejudicing my opinion."

"Curious" was Giles's comment.

"Decidedly so," I said. "Now the thing I need to do is question them. Do you think they'll be amenable to my playing the nosey parker with them?"

"I can't see that they would object too vociferously," Giles said. "It's the prime topic of conversation anyway." He glanced at his watch. "*Tempus fugit,* and all that. It's nearly time for tea." He pressed a bell on one side of the desk, and less than two minutes later, Thompson appeared.

"Yes, Sir Giles?"

"Thompson, I believe we'll have tea here in the library. And if you would be so good as to ask all of our guests to join me here." He smiled wolfishly. "And, Thompson, there's a good fellow. Do your best to let them understand, without actually saying so, of course, that I would construe it as the gravest insult should they fail to appear."

Thompson inclined his head and disappeared.

Giles laughed. "Once Thompson is through with them, they won't dare not show up for tea."

"And here the spider sits," I said, "spinning his web."

Chapter Twenty-One

Within twenty minutes after Thompson's departure, not only had the tea tray arrived, but so had Piers Limpley, Dittany Harwood, Moira Rhys-Morgan, and Cliff Weatherstone. The suspects had gathered in the library, and I was prepared to launch into my best Poirot imitation.

I told Giles of the stratagem I had employed with Jessamy Cholmondley-Pease, that I was going to write a true crime book about the murder, and I decided that same gambit might work just as well for the purposes of the forthcoming interview.

For the first few minutes after the four chief suspects had arrived, Giles, the very essence of the proper host, kept them busy, serving them tea and seeing them comfortably settled around the informal circle of chairs we had set up. Once they all had tea and biscuits, I cleared my throat and saw their attention focus on me.

"I asked Sir Giles to call you all together for tea," I said in my most unctuous tones, "because I am going to prevail upon your goodwill to assist me in a project that I am planning to undertake." I shot a quick, meaning glance at

Cliff Weatherstone to alert him. He caught the signal and winked to show that he was ready to play along.

"You are all aware, of course, that I am a writer, a historian by training. Though my work thus far has been confined to illuminating the distant past," I said mendaciously, "in particular the time period known as the Middle Ages, I have decided it is time for a change." Their eyes were already glazing over, but I was about to startle them completely awake. "I plan to write a book about the sad events of the past few days."

I raised a hand to stifle the beginnings of mumbling and grumbling. "I realize that you will doubtless think this is in questionable taste, but I would also beg you to consider for the moment how much more palatable it will be in the long run for you to have someone sympathetic, someone who has already met you, rather than a complete stranger, write the book that must inevitably follow this regrettable occurrence."

As I paused to gauge their reactions, I reflected that I most likely would write about Harwood's murder, but in the guise of Diana Dorchester, that new maven of the English village mystery who would one day make her debut. There was, however, no need to tell them this.

Cliff Weatherstone smiled at me, as if congratulating me on my stratagem to get them all to talk. Moira Rhys-Morgan regarded me blankly, whereas Piers Limpley and Dittany Harwood cast more calculating gazes at me.

"If any of you should choose not to talk to me," I said, "I shall quite understand. My task would therefore be more difficult, requiring more *speculation* on my part. But that, naturally, could not be helped in such a case."

The word "speculation" made them a bit uneasy, I could see. I paused to let them think about it for a moment.

Cliff Weatherstone spoke. "I can't say that I'm totally

enamored of the idea of anyone writing such a book, Professor, but I know you're right. Someone undoubtedly will, and it might as well be someone we can trust to be fair."

Dittany Harwood regarded him with eyes thinned to the merest slits as she sipped her tea. Replacing the cup in its saucer, she set them down on a small table next her chair. "I'm with Cliff, Professor. I'd rather no one wrote such a book, as you might imagine, but I know it's inevitable. My poor brother was far too well known, and the public will be hungry for details of his murder."

Her tone was so detached, she might have been speaking of the day's shopping. "What would you like to know?" She turned to me and fixed me with a bland, innocent gaze.

"Thank you, Miss Harwood. I appreciate your willingness to cooperate. It goes without saying, I'm sure, that the innocent have little to fear from this project." That was a lie, and they all knew it, because even the innocent among them would have secrets they preferred to keep from public view. But murder will out, as the Bard of Stratford-upon-Avon said.

I pulled a notebook from my pocket and sat down. "First, I think, I'd like to get fixed in my mind the hour or so before we found the body. I have a rough idea of the sequence of some of the events of that time period, but it would be best to have as complete a picture as possible."

I flipped open the notebook and pretended to consult something written there. "Mrs. Rhys-Morgan, you told us last night that you had spoken with Mr. Harwood at roughly seven-twenty, and he told you that he planned to do a bit of work in the drawing room. Is that correct?"

Moira frowned at me. "If the others are going along with this farce, I suppose I have no choice. Yes, I suppose it was about that time that I spoke with Zeke." Her voice caught in a strangled half-sob upon the name of the victim. She paused to regain control of herself. "Zeke said he wanted some time alone in the room to rethink the colors he had chosen."

"We had already decided the colors," Dittany interrupted, her annoyance evident. "I can't imagine why he would have wanted to change them at that stage in the process."

Moira shrugged, then cast a sideways glance at Giles. "I believe it might have had something to do with Lady Prunella and her anxieties over the red paint. Zeke seemed quite intent upon getting back at her for what had happened earlier in the day."

Giles wisely kept silent, and I was thankful that Lady Prunella was not present. Her fluttering would have derailed any attempt to question the group after that announcement.

"When you spoke with Mr. Harwood," I said, "where were you?"

Moira colored faintly. "In his room. We, ah, had some personal matters to discuss, and it was as I was leaving him that he mentioned his plans."

I thought about pressing her to explain the nature of the "personal matters," but from her evident embarrassment, I had a good idea as to what those matters had been. I turned instead to Piers Limpley, who eyed me rather as would a rat confronted by a python.

"Now, Mr. Limpley, I believe you spoke with Harwood right after that? Say, at about seven twenty-five?"

He cleared his throat. "As far as I can remember, yes, it was about that time. I had stopped by his room to remind him of the time we were to gather in the library." He offered a prim smile. "Zeke had rather a casual attitude toward time, and I was always having to try to keep him on schedule."

"How long did this conversation last?" I had my pen poised to make a notation.

"No more than two minutes," Piers said, after reflecting. "And then?"

"I went to my room to get ready for dinner," Piers said. "I needed time to relax for a few minutes and to change clothes."

I flipped a page in the notebook, staring down at the diagram there. While we had waited for the suspects to arrive in the library, Giles had quickly sketched for me a small floor plan to show me who was occupying which bedroom. "I believe your room was directly across the hall from Harwood's."

"That is correct," Piers said.

"Mrs. Rhys-Morgan is in the room next to Harwood, and Miss Harwood, you are in the next room after that. Mr. Weatherstone, I believe you are in the last room, just after Miss Harwood. Correct?" I looked up at them.

They all nodded.

"Did anyone see Harwood go downstairs to the drawing room?" I asked.

They all shook their heads.

"Where were each of you, then, at approximately seven-thirty?" I looked at each of them in turn, and each of them answered, "In my room."

"You were all in your rooms, and presumably Harwood was in the drawing room, at seven-thirty or shortly thereafter. Right." I looked up at Giles. "And Giles, where were you?"

"In my room, reading. I was already dressed for dinner." He looked for a moment as if he might continue, but he fell silent instead. I would come back to that later. I wondered what he was reluctant to tell me.

"I, of course, was at home," I said, flashing a friendly smile. I settled back in my chair and regarded them all for a long moment. "Now, we get to the tricky part. We must examine the time period in which it was most likely that Harwood was killed."

I paused to let that sink in, then consulted my notebook again. "According to what I have been told by Lady Prunella, it would have been five or six minutes after Harwood went downstairs to the drawing room that she confronted him there." I looked up. "I don't suppose any of you saw her go downstairs?"

Piers Limpley frowned. "How could we have, Professor? According to what I have heard, Lady Prunella made use of some sort of secret staircase to go downstairs and spy upon poor Zeke."

So they had heard about the staircase. "Ah, yes, you are quite right, Mr. Limpley. Lady Prunella did indeed go downstairs by way of those stairs. Did any of you happen to see her enter Harwood's bedroom?"

Again, the answer was in the negative.

"To resume, then," I said. "Again, according to Lady Prunella, she was with Harwood for approximately five or six minutes, after having watched him through a peephole for some three or four minutes. That brings us to roughly seven forty-two, when Lady Prunella left the drawing room. She came straight to the library, whereupon she fortified herself with a brandy and remained here. She did not leave this room again until we all left, as a group, to discover the body of Harwood in the drawing room."

No one commented, though I paused invitingly. I plowed on. "Giles and Mr. Weatherstone were the first to arrive in the library, after Lady Prunella. What time would you estimate that to have been, Giles?"

"Perhaps two or three minutes before eight o'clock," Giles said, his face impassive.

"Mrs. Rhys-Morgan, I believe you arrived right after that?"

Moira nodded at me.

"Mr. Limpley, Miss Harwood, you arrived together, a few minutes after Mrs. Rhys-Morgan?"

Dittany yawned. "Yes, it was three or four minutes after eight, I'm afraid. I had heard a clock chiming somewhere upstairs before I was quite ready to leave my room. When I stepped out into the hall a couple of minutes later, Piers was just coming out of his room, and we walked down together."

"And how long after that, would you say, was it before I arrived?" I remembered it as being close to ten minutes after eight when I had walked into the library.

"No more than four or five minutes, perhaps," Piers said.

"Thank you," I said. "I think I have all that reasonably clear in my mind." I tapped the notebook against one knee. "Now we must, of course, zero in on the brief time period in which the killer must have struck. I refer, naturally, to the quarter hour, give or take a couple of minutes, *after* Lady Prunella left Harwood in the drawing room and *before* you all began arriving in the library just before dinner."

I had been focusing on each of them at random, trying to get a reading on their emotions. With the exception of Moira Rhys-Morgan, though, I had come up blank. She was obviously in distress, seemingly upset over Harwood's murder, while the other three remained cool and watchful. If one of them were guilty, he or she must be a killer poker player.

"What about Lady Prunella?" Moira spoke in harsh tones. "We have only her word for it that Zeke was alive when she left him."

Giles jerked in his chair, but I forestalled him. "Yes, as you say, we have only her word for it. She has no alibi for the probable time of the murder, either, unless it occurred while we were all in the library waiting in vain for Harwood to appear."

Giles frowned in distaste at that thought, and I couldn't blame him. It was rather a horrible thought, that a man might have died by violence while we were complaining of his tardiness.

"That must have been what happened, Professor, if Lady Prunella is indeed innocent. I certainly can't think of a reason for her to have done it," Dittany said, leaning forward in her chair. "The murder *must* have taken place while we were all in the library."

"Why are you so certain, Miss Harwood?" I asked. Indeed, her voice had carried firm conviction.

"Because, if Lady Prunella *didn't* do it," she said smugly, "the rest of us couldn't have. We all have alibis."

Chapter Twenty-Two

Piers Limpley nodded vigorously once Dittany had made her triumphant announcement. "Yes, that's right," he said, his voice almost squeaking with excitement. "We all have alibis."

"How lucky for you," I said. Now I was about to hear whatever it was that Robin Chase had wanted me to evaluate. What could their alibis be? Had they all been together in one room, playing cards?

"I'll go first, shall I?" Dittany said, and without waiting for anyone's assent, she plunged ahead. "I was in my room at seven-thirty, and I was in the midst of getting dressed for dinner, when the telephone rang. It must have been about, oh, seven-fortyish when it rang, because I had finished touching up my face and was about to start on my hair."

She beamed at me, very pleased with herself and her story. "As I was saying, the phone rang, and I answered, thinking it was probably Zeke or Piers wanting something done at the last minute. But it wasn't. It was my flatmate in London, ringing me from our flat while she was waiting for her boyfriend to meet her. He—the boyfriend, that is—

is always running late, so Paula—that's my flatmate—decided to call me and find out how things were going here in the wilds of Bedfordshire. She's never been north of London, can you believe it?"

I forbore to answer what I considered a rhetorical question and instead asked a question of my own. "How long were you on the phone with your friend?"

"Oh, until nearly eight o'clock," Dittany said, clearly pleased. "That's why I was running a bit late, getting downstairs to meet everyone in the library. I lost all track of time while Paula and I were nattering on. That always happens when the two of us get going." She giggled. "Drives her boyfriend mad, it does, but then he should be on time, shouldn't he? Or else Paula wouldn't be calling me to chat so much. But I finally thought of the time, and anyway Paula's boyfriend had just showed up, so I rang off and hurried to finish my hair and get dressed."

I regarded her in silence for a moment. Something about her demeanor made my nose twitch, metaphorically, that is. She seemed inordinately pleased with herself. Her alibi was elaborately simple, if you'll pardon the oxymoron.

"And I suppose Paula will be able to corroborate your story?"

"Of course," Dittany said, not taking the least umbrage from my rather testy question. "That puts me in the clear, doesn't it? After all, the police would only have to check the phone records, wouldn't they?"

If she were telling the truth, she would be in the clear, I reflected. A check of the phone records would reveal whether a call had been made from the flat in London to Blitherington Hall, certainly, and how long the conversation had lasted.

It was all so easy, it must be true.

"Yes, the police can, and probably will, check all that," I said.

"Oh yes, the detective inspector said they would." Dittany frowned suddenly. "But the only problem is that Paula and her boyfriend left this morning for a two-week holiday in southern Spain, and I haven't the foggiest where they're staying or how to reach them."

"Doesn't one of them have a mobile?" I asked sardonically.

Dittany responded with an arch look. "Ah, no, Paula always leaves hers behind. Doesn't want anyone from the solicitor's office where she works trying to call her, she says."

"Then I suppose it will take a couple of weeks until the police can corroborate your alibi," I said. "Unless, of course, they enlist the aid of the Spanish police in tracking down Paula and her boyfriend."

Dittany frowned slightly at that. Then she shrugged. "*Qué será, será,* as they say in Spain."

"*Creo que sí,*" I said. " 'I believe so,' as they also say in Spain. Well, that disposes of Miss Harwood. Mr. Limpley, your turn. What is your alibi?"

"Actually, Professor," Piers said, his tone quavering a bit as he spoke, "it's not simply *my* alibi. It's rather a matter of *our* alibi." He tapered off into an odd silence.

"Do you mean you were with someone during the time in question?" I asked.

He nodded.

"Well, speak up, man. Who was it?"

"Piers is being a gentleman, Professor," Moira Rhys-Morgan said, and I inferred from her tone in addressing me that I was anything but. "He was with me from about seven-forty until about five minutes to eight."

Piers, relieved, nodded eagerly. "Yes, that's it, Professor. I hadn't wanted to speak without Moira's consent."

I couldn't see that such delicacy of feeling was called for, unless they had been engaged in some less-than-delicate activity during the time in question. I sought a tactful way to voice that thought.

"Unless you were engaged in a plan to make away with the Blitherington family silver, I can't see any difficulty in admitting to such an alibi," I said, attempting to make light of it.

Moira sniffed in distaste. "If you must know, and I see that you must, Professor, I was in considerable distress. Zeke and I had not parted on the most amicable of terms, when I had left his room, and Piers was doing his best to dissuade me from leaving Blitherington Hall that evening. Indeed, I had decided to go back to London and seek another job." She looked down at her hands. "Piers did not totally dissuade me from that plan, although he did convince me not to leave that evening. I had planned to leave for London the next morning."

This was certainly an interesting development, particularly given what Cliff Weatherstone had told me about the nature of the relationship between Moira and Zeke. Not to mention the long-suffering Piers, with his unrequited love of Moira. I examined the two of them for a moment. One of them could have killed Harwood, and the other was covering it up. It was just possible.

"If I might ask," I said, addressing Piers, "how did you come to know of Mrs. Rhys-Morgan's distress?"

"From Zeke" was the unhappy answer. Piers cut a glance toward his beloved. "I'm afraid I wasn't entirely truthful with you before. I did stop by Zeke's room to remind him of the time we were to meet in the library for dinner, and I did so. But then Zeke went off on a tirade against Moira, and I gathered that Moira was extremely upset and threatening to quit. I said some rather cutting things to Zeke, but of course he paid not the slightest attention." His voice rose in indignation. "He never took me seriously." His shoulders slumped. "I went to my room and waited a few minutes, until I was sure Zeke had gone downstairs. Then I went to Moira's room to talk to her."

"I see," I said. "And do you agree with Mrs. Rhys-Morgan's estimate of the time you were together?"

He nodded vigorously.

"In that case, I suppose you're in the clear also," I said. "It's a pity, however, that no one else saw you go in or come out of Mrs. Rhys-Morgan's room, or saw the two of you together."

Moira bristled with indignation, but Piers simply looked resigned.

"Ah, Simon?"

Cliff Weatherstone claimed my attention. "Yes, Cliff?"

"I believe I can corroborate at least part of Piers's alibi," he said, and he did not appear particularly happy to be doing so.

"How so?"

"Because I saw Piers come out of the bedroom at approximately five minutes to eight."

"Ah," I said. "And where were you at the time? Coming out of your bedroom?"

"Not exactly," he said, casting a glance sideways at Giles.

"Oh, for heaven's sake," Giles said impatiently. "Don't be such a pillock, Cliff." He stared at me. "Cliff was in my room, Simon, and had been for nearly twenty minutes. We were on the point of leaving to come down to the library. That's when Cliff saw Mr. Limpley, although he had neglected to mention that to me."

"I thought you were reading in your room," I said coolly.

"I was," Giles acknowledged, "until Cliff knocked on my door."

"And the two of you were just chatting away during this time, I suppose."

Giles reddened slightly. "More or less."

That was such a patent lie I forbore to comment. So Giles and Cliff were in Giles's bedroom, making out, to put it as politely as possible, during those important fifteen minutes. Well, bully for them to have such a spiffing alibi.

Normally, I am in complete control of my emotions, and what happened next frightened me. I was seized with such a rage that I literally saw red. I saw the red of Cliff Weatherstone's blood spurting from his neck, the neck I longed to rip from the rest of his body.

The vision was so strong that, for a moment, I thought I must have attacked Cliff. A squeak of alarm came from someone, most likely Piers Limpley, and the haze of red began to recede. As I regained my composure, I could see that everyone in the room had drawn back in alarm.

Good grief, I thought. What on earth had they seen?

And swift upon that, another thought: What the bloody hell was going on with me?

"I beg your pardon," I said, a trifle shaky. "I fear that all this has given me rather a fierce headache."

Giles stared at me as if I were someone he had never met. "Is there anything you need, Simon?"

"No, no, Giles," I said. "No need to worry. I often get these headaches, and fortunately they usually pass quickly." Lucky for Cliff Weatherstone, I thought bleakly. If this so-called "attack" hadn't passed, I might have done him fatal damage.

I sat back in my chair and closed my notebook with a snap. "All of this is most interesting. It looks rather as if you are all in the clear—if your alibis hold up." I shook my head in puzzlement. "That must mean, then, someone from outside the house somehow got into the drawing room and murdered poor Mr. Harwood."

The relief I felt emanating from several of them was almost palpable. But underlying it all was a thin thread of anxiety. One of them, perhaps more, was worried about something. But what?

"Very interesting indeed," I said, standing up, "and quite a puzzle, worthy of the combined talents of Hercule Poirot and Miss Marple. If you will all be so kind as to excuse me, I think I had better be off home, to let my head have a bit of rest and recover from this headache. Thank you all for your cooperation."

Giles got up from his chair and followed me to the door. "Are you certain you're quite all right, Simon? I've never seen you look so dashed odd. I thought for a moment you were going to go berserk and have a go at one of us."

"I'm fine, Giles," I lied, "just tired. I've been working too hard, I suppose." I didn't want to look him in the eye. After what had passed between us just a short time before, I didn't want to think any further about what he and Cliff had been doing in his bedroom. "Go back to your guests."

"Well, if you're sure, Simon," he said, his voice and his manner still evincing his concern.

"I'm sure," I said, opening the door. "I'll talk to you later."

He stood in the doorway, watching as I made a hasty exit from Blitherington Hall. I couldn't get out of there fast enough.

I gunned the Jag down the driveway, scaring the daylights out of several members of the press who dallied a bit too long before getting out of my way. I reached home long before they could catch up with me, and I locked myself inside, away from their inquisitiveness.

I went upstairs to the bathroom, opened the cabinet, and pulled out my bottle of pills. I stood there staring at them for a very long time, wondering. Tristan Lovelace had told me I had merely gotten hold of a weak batch.

I wondered.

Chapter Twenty-Three

I stood staring down at the pills in my hand, my thoughts racing. Paranoia wasn't one of my usual traits, but I feared I might be succumbing to it now.

Had someone tampered with my pills?

Why would someone tamper with my pills?

Revenge was the most likely answer to that second question. I could think of only one person who might bear me that much ill will.[*]

For someone to tamper with my pills, that person would have to understand the nature of the pills and the "condition" for which they were prescribed.

Possession of that knowledge fit the profile of the person I considered my nemesis.

How had it been done?

It had to have been done recently, within the past few days. Someone could have sneaked into Laurel Cottage and tampered with the pills, I supposed, while I was in the village on an errand. Certainly it hadn't happened at night,

---

[*]Author's note: Kindly remember, if you will, the events recounted in *Posted to Death,* and no doubt you will reach the same conclusion that I have.

when I was ostensibly asleep, like the rest of the village, because I would have sensed the presence of any other creature in the cottage.

I spent most nights, when others would be sleeping, working at my computer. I did tend to become rather absorbed in my work, often losing track of time, but I hadn't thought I could be so oblivious that I wouldn't sense an alien presence somewhere in the house.

Perhaps I was wrong.

I decided I needed to examine the pills more carefully. I carried them downstairs and into my office. I cleared some space on the desk and rolled the pills out onto the blotter. I pulled a lamp closer and switched it on, then retrieved a magnifying glass from one of the desk drawers.

Picking up one pill after another, I examined each of them with great care. As I worked, I sorted them into two groups. When I had finished, there were eleven pills in one group and about thirty in the other.

The added light had irritated my eyes, and I switched the lamp off as quickly as I could. But the combination of the bright light and the magnifying glass had allowed me see that there were two different kinds of pills in the bottle. Both kinds had a squiggled logo etched on them, but in the group of eleven, the squiggle was a tiny bit shorter. They were all of uniform size, color, and shape. It was the logo that made them subtly different.

The question now was, which group was the real thing? And which was the fake?

I had never examined the pills that closely before, so I wasn't sure which group of pills bore the authentic logo. I thought perhaps it was the group of eleven that were the authentic pills.

I remembered the small pillbox I kept in my jacket whenever I went out—my emergency supply. When was the last time I had put pills in it? I thought back. Nearly a week ago, I decided. Before the tampering had taken place, as far as I could determine.

I went upstairs to retrieve the pillbox from my dressing table. Back downstairs again, I examined the six pills contained in the ornately enameled snuffbox I had adapted for use as a pillbox. All six had the same shorter logo as the eleven pills I had decided were probably authentic.

I got an envelope from the desk and put the fakes inside, sealing it. I would send the fakes to the chemist in London and ask him to test them. In the meantime, I had enough of the authentic pills to make do until a fresh batch arrived tomorrow.

For good measure, I popped one of the pills into my mouth and swallowed. I'd have to put my theory to the test, I decided. I would find an attractive neck, stare at it for a moment, and see whether I had the urge to bite it.

Very funny, I thought, as I picked up the phone and dialed a number I had now memorized. "Yes, is Detective Inspector Chase available?" I listened for a moment. "I see. Then will you please ask him to ring Professor Kirby-Jones at his earliest convenience? I have some important information for him related to his present murder inquiry. Yes, thank you." I rang off.

I was taking a risk, I knew, by getting in touch with Robin Chase. I intended to ask him to come to Laurel Cottage, and if he came, his would be the neck with which I'd test myself. I needed to talk to him, anyway, and as for my little test, well, *qué será, será,* as Dittany Harwood had put it.

While I waited for Robin to ring me back, I sat and thought about the agent employed by Nemesis, as I preferred to call my adversary in the matter of the pills. It hadn't taken me long to finger the culprit, so to speak. I remembered finding Violet Glubb coming out of my bathroom. I also remembered how Vi had appeared so providentially on my doorstep in answer to my ad.

Where were her references? I wondered suddenly. She had given me a few sheets of paper, which consisted of two brief letters written by former employers and a list of her most recent situations. I dug around on the desk and finally found what I was seeking lodged beneath a few chapters of the latest Daphne Deepwood opus.

The phone rang, claiming my attention. "Hello. Ah yes, Robin, how good of you to ring me back so quickly. I say, can you possibly drop by for a bit? I'd like to talk to you about what I learned this afternoon at Blitherington Hall." I listened for a moment. "Great. Thanks, Robin, I'll see you in a few minutes." I rang off.

I picked up Vi's references again. I read through the two letters of recommendation, both of which appeared perfectly legitimate. I had meant to get in touch with the two women who had written them, but somehow I had never done so. I tended to rely on my own judgments of people anyway, and usually this had served me well.

I thought back to one notable exception, however, and now it seemed I had been hoist with my own petard. I had underestimated Nemesis then . . . and now.

Reaching for the phone, I dialed the number of one of Vi's references, that of a Mrs. Polly Charles. A childish voice answered, and I asked to speak to Mrs. Charles. The receiver on the other end thumped down upon some hard surface, and I winced. A couple of minutes later, a harassed-sounding voice gasped into my ear.

"Hello. Is this Mrs. Polly Charles of Abingdon?"

"Yes. You're not selling something, are you? Because I really do not have the time to listen. The children are rather clamoring for something to eat, and I'm much too busy—"

The voice would have continued rambling, I had no doubt, if I had not ruthlessly, and rudely, cut in. "No, Mrs. Charles, I'm not selling anything. I'm calling to speak with you about—"

"Gemma, put that down. At once, do you hear me? Gemma, listen to Mummy, please, and put that down!" I could hear the voice of a child whining in the background, before Mrs. Charles turned her attention back to me. "I'm sorry, you were saying?"

"Yes, Mrs. Charles, I am calling to inquire about a letter of reference you wrote for Violet Glubb. Did you indeed write Violet such a letter?"

"Gemma, no, I said. Not now. In a minute. Wait till Mummy finishes talking on the phone. Um, yes, I did write a letter for Vi. She was such a treasure, and so good with the children. I quite hated to see her leave. No, Gemma!"

I suspected that Gemma must have had something to do with Vi's desire to leave the Charles household. She sounded like a perfectly dreadful child.

"Then you found her dependable and trustworthy?" I thought I had better ask what I wanted as quickly as possible, before Gemma destroyed the house.

"Oh, my, yes," Mrs. Charles said. "She was with me for nearly three years. Mind you, she did have some peculiar ideas about children. I once caught her making Gemma sit in a corner by herself. I told her she mustn't thwart Gemma's creative expression, but she didn't understand."

I held the phone away from my ear as, once again, Mrs. Charles exhorted Gemma—completely in vain, I was certain—not to do whatever it was she was doing.

When the noise on the other end subsided slightly, I risked another question. "Then you know nothing, really, of a detrimental nature about her? You would recommend my employing her?"

"Oh yes," Mrs. Charles said, a bit out of breath. I had a

sudden vision of her having had to chase Gemma down from the top of some tall piece of furniture. "Everything was fine. That is, until Vi also began working for that rather odd woman who moved in down the road about seven or eight months ago."

"Oh, really," I said, trying to sound casual, though I knew I was on to something important with this bit of news. "Odd, you say. How is she odd?"

"Gemma, darling, just a minute longer, please. Gemma!" The receiver thumped down, and I thought the connection had been severed. But in a moment Mrs. Charles, still short of breath, picked it up and resumed our conversation, such as it was. "Odd? Oh, my, yes. Do you know, none of us has ever seen her during the daytime? She says she has some sort of allergic reaction to the sun. Rather potty, it sounds to me, but then, people are allergic to all sorts of strange things these days."

Bingo! I had found Nemesis.

"And what is this woman's name, Mrs. Charles?"

"It's Wickham. That's all I know. Never heard anyone call her anything but Mrs. Wickham. She's a widow, I believe. Quite attractive, really. It's a wonder she's never married again. Gemma!"

Figuring I had gained as much information from Mrs. Charles as I could before Gemma brought down the house in her attempts to express herself creatively, I hastily thanked her and rang off.

I picked up the second letter of reference, and there it was, cool as you please. Signed "Mrs. J. Wickham, Abingdon."

Now that I understood the nature of the threat, I felt much better. I had the measure of Mrs. J. Wickham, and I would take steps to spike her guns. She was clever, I'd give her that, but then, so was I.

The doorbell rang, interrupting my plans for exacting

my counter-revenge. I went to the door to admit Robin
Chase, who was a bit bedraggled from the rain now cours-
ing down.

"Robin, do come in and dry yourself. What a beastly
night. I was so busy with work I hadn't even noticed it was
raining." I took his coat and hung it on the rack in the
hall.

"How about some tea to warm you?" I asked as I led
him into the sitting room. "Or, better yet, how about a tot
of whisky? Are you on duty?"

"Whisky sounds fine, Simon, with a dash of soda, if you
don't mind." He sat down in his usual chair, looking tired
and damp around the edges.

I handed him his whisky and soda, then gestured to the
humidor. "And do help yourself to a cigar, Robin, if you
like. I think you could do with a bit of relaxing."

"Don't mind if I do," Robin said, reaching for the humidor. "Yes, I've not had much sleep since the case began."

I waited until he had his cigar burning to his satisfaction
before relating to him my tea-time interview with the chief
suspects. I concluded by saying, "If their alibis hold up,
then I'm afraid you will have to be on the lookout for a
killer who somehow sneaked in from outside."

"What did you make of their stories, Simon? Did they
seem to be telling the truth?"

I shrugged. "Their stories are all so simple and so ordinary, it seems hard to believe they're not the truth. But
they're also dashed convenient, don't you think?"

Robin nodded. "I took each of them through their stories at least five times, and they never deviated significantly
from the first time they told me. If there's a hole in any of
them, I've not yet found it."

"One possibility that occurred to me is that Piers Limpley
and Moira Rhys-Morgan are lying about having spent the
time together. According to Cliff Weatherstone, Limpley is

desperately in love with Mrs. Rhys-Morgan, and I suppose it's conceivable that he would lie to protect her. I'm not so sure she would lie to protect him, though she does seem to be fond of him."

Robin nodded. "I had a go at breaking down their story, but they wouldn't budge. It would help if we could find the murder weapon, or weapons, I should say. But no luck thus far."

"The only one of them without an alibi is Lady Prunella."

"And we have only her word for it that Harwood was alive when she left him in the drawing room." Robin drew on his cigar and expelled the smoke in a frustrated burst. "I simply cannot see Lady Prunella as the murderer, Simon."

"No, I agree," I said. "It would help also if we knew how the murderer gained access to the drawing room. Was it by means of that secret staircase, or did Harwood let his killer into the room through the door?"

"No clear answer to that either," Robin said glumly. "I've questioned the staff several times over, and none of them was in that bloody hallway during that time period. They were busy preparing for dinner, and they went in and out of the dining room, but they don't have to use the hallway for that."

"Was the front door unlocked?"

"Thompson can't remember for sure. He thinks it probably was, but he can't swear to it. The man's eighty if he's a day, and his memory is a bit sketchy at times." Robin sighed through a cloud of smoke.

"Then someone could have sneaked in through the front door, I suppose," I said. "Robin, what do you know about Jessamy Cholmondley-Pease?"

"Nothing to make me suspect that she's involved in this, Simon. Why do you ask?"

"Did Jessamy tell you that I found her lurking in the bushes outside the Hall the night of the murder?"

"What? No, she bloody well didn't, Simon, and neither did you."

"Sorry about that, Robin," I said, a bit embarrassed. "I really thought I had." Before he could censure me further, I hastened to enlighten him.

"Lost jewelry, eh?" Robin laughed. "How many times have I heard that one?"

"I think Jessamy bears further investigation, Robin. Did you know her father had been gardener at Blitherington Hall? Name of Macleod, and apparently he was quite chummy with Giles's grandfather. Giles also told me that our Jessamy has a bit of a checkered past. Ran off to London when she was a teenager, then came back here about fifteen years ago, when she snared Cholmondley-Pease."

As I waited for Robin to chew over these facts, I suddenly realized that I hadn't once been tempted to bite him on the neck. I had been right, then, about which batch of pills were the real thing. I was much relieved.

"You think it's possible she might have known Harwood in London?" Robin asked doubtfully.

"I know it's a bit of a long shot," I said, "but at this stage, what can it hurt to do a bit of digging?"

While Robin smoked in silence, mulling that over, I thought of something else I should mention. Before I could give voice to my thought, however, I heard the sounds of a key turning in the lock at the front door.

"Excuse me a moment, Robin," I said, rising from the sofa. "I believe there's someone at the front door."

"No need to get up on my account, Simon," Giles said from the doorway. "My, my, how cozy we are this evening. I do beg your pardon for interrupting your little rendezvous."

Chapter Twenty-Four

"Really, Giles, don't just stand there dripping all over the floor. Take off your coat and hang it up in the hallway, if you please."

The last thing I needed right now was Giles having a fit of jealousy in front of Robin. Especially given the fact that he was Cliff Weatherstone's alibi for the murder of Zeke Harwood. I was still inclined to see a bit of red over that little item of news. It served him right to see me here with Robin, since I had found him with Cliff Weatherstone on several occasions.

I poured Giles a whisky and soda and refilled Robin's glass as well. I handed Giles the glass when he had stalked back into the room. He tossed it off in one gulp, then handed it back to me. "Once more, please, Simon," he said, having the grace to appear slightly abashed as he seated himself on the sofa.

"Very well," I said. I prepared the drink, then carried it to him. I too sat on the sofa, but at the other end.

"Simon and I were discussing the case, Giles," Robin said mildly. "Actually, you arrived at a most opportune time, for there's something I've been meaning to ask you."

I wondered whether Giles had noted that Robin had not, for once, called him "Sir Giles."

Giles's eyes narrowed as he sipped his whisky. "What would that be, Detective Inspector?"

I wanted to smack him. Just when I thought he was giving over some of his juvenile behavior, he persisted in acting like a spoiled child.

Robin, however, remained undaunted. "It's about this secret stairway of yours. Is there any other access to it, besides the doors in the drawing room and the bedroom above?"

"Yes, there's a cellar beneath it. Didn't I tell you that?"

Giles had told me, but I had forgotten about it, I must admit.

With a small frown, Robin replied, his tone still mild, "No, I don't believe you did."

"Can't believe I didn't mention it," Giles said carelessly. "Still, I can't see that it matters. It hasn't been opened in years."

"That you know of," Robin pointed out.

"Well, yes," Giles said. "But surely you would have seen signs of it, when you and your minions examined it."

"The SOCOs did a very thorough job, I can assure you," Robin said, his voice at last taking on a bit of an edge. "But it would certainly have been a great help to have known about this cellar before now."

"Sorry," Giles muttered, accepting the rebuke more mildly than I would have expected.

"How big is this cellar?" Robin asked. "And is there a way into the cellar, other than from this stairway?"

"It's a glorified priest hole," Giles said. "I believe one of my ancestors used it to hide his brandy back during the

Napoleonic wars, and before that it might have been used as a priest hole. One of the Blitheringtons was a Catholic holdout for a while, if memory serves. But then we all became good little Anglicans, don't you know.

"I suppose there must be another way in and out of the bally thing, but I don't know where it is. I thought my grandfather had had it blocked off, because one of the grooms in those days was sneaking in and having it off with my grandmother." He grinned. "Which could explain why the old bat was so dashed unpleasant when I knew her. Hard to imagine her having illicit trysts with a groom, right under the old man's nose, so to speak."

Robin set his empty glass on the table in front of him and stubbed out his cigar. He stood up. "I'm afraid I must ask you, then, to accompany me back to Blitherington Hall, Sir Giles. I think we should examine this secret cellar as quickly as possible. I don't know that the killer used it, but we had best make certain. If I might use your phone, Simon, I'll have to get my team moving."

"Certainly, Robin," I said. "Use the phone in my office."

I waited until Robin was out of earshot before I spoke my mind to Giles. "Really, Giles, I despair of you. How could you behave so childishly just now?"

"I'm sorry, Simon," Giles said, and indeed he did appear contrite. "I came here with the best intentions, but when I saw you with Chase, all that flew out the window." He clenched his hands into fists. "You really do drive me mad sometimes, Simon."

He took a deep breath to steady himself. "I came here because I wanted to explain to you about Cliff Weatherstone, Simon. It's not what you think—his alibi, I mean."

"You mean to say you weren't snogging in your bedroom?" I used the slang deliberately.

Giles's face colored. "Not exactly."

"What do you mean, Giles? How does one 'not exactly' snog?"

"I mean," he said, "that Cliff certainly wanted to, even tried to, but I wouldn't. We had a bit of an argument, if you must know, and it was over you."

"You resisted Cliff's considerable wiles for my sake?" I said. "I am truly honored."

The sarcasm was uncalled for, I knew, but I couldn't seem to stop myself. I had to admit to myself that I was just as jealous as Giles was. "Sorry, Giles, that was unworthy of me. Forgive me."

"If you'll do the same for me." His smile was radiant.

Robin cleared his throat from the doorway. "If you don't mind, Sir Giles," he said, "I think we had best get back to Blitherington Hall. My team is on the way."

I wondered how much of that little exchange Robin might have heard. Not too much, I hoped.

"Mind if I tag along, Robin?" I said. "I'd love to see this secret staircase, if I might."

"Why not?" Robin shrugged.

"Thanks." I turned to Giles. "Did you walk here, Giles?"

He nodded.

"That's why you were so wet when you arrived here. You can come with me, then, and we'll follow Robin in his car."

And thus we set off for Blitherington Hall.

It was certainly a dark and stormy night. No wonder, then, that Giles had been out of sorts by the time he slogged through all that, only to find me, warm and comfortable and enjoying the company of the man he considered his chief rival for my affections. Silly boy, I thought fondly, as I concentrated on directing the Jag through the driving rain.

"Do you have any clue as to who the murderer is, Simon?" Giles asked, stirring in the seat beside me.

"There are several possibilities, Giles," I said. "Much depends on who's telling the truth . . . and who's not. But there's also a bit of an unknown factor." I was thinking, in the latter case, of Jessamy Cholmondley-Pease. She had played some role in this little drama, but what that was, I wasn't completely certain.

"And my mother is the only one who doesn't have some sort of alibi," Giles said. "Still, I can't think that Chase is going to arrest her."

"No, I don't think he'll do that," I said as I drew the car into the forecourt of Blitherington Hall and parked behind Robin, who was just getting out of his car. The press had at last decamped, apparently not brave enough—or fool-hardy enough—to sit through the rain tonight.

We made a dash for the front door. Robin stood aside to allow Giles in first. Thompson had neglected to lock the door, which made Giles's key unnecessary. And if Thompson had left the front door unlocked on a night like this, might he not also have left it unlocked the evening of the murder? Just last night, I realized with a start. Yes, he might well have done so, which only complicated matters.

"The SOCOs will be here in a few minutes," Robin said, taking off his wet coat. We hung ours alongside his on the rack, then followed him to the door of the drawing room. Robin drew the key from his pocket. "I had thought to return this to you, Sir Giles," he said, brandishing the key, "but it seems I might need it a bit longer." He opened the door.

We stepped inside. The lights had been left burning, and I paused to glance around the room. It did indeed resemble a shambles. Surely Harwood's crew would come in and clean up their mess, despite the fact that this was a job that would remain unfinished. That would be the decent thing to do. They would at least retrieve their tools and supplies, if nothing else.

Robin directed our attention to the wall where the door to the hidden staircase stood slightly ajar. "I'd rather that you not go all the way inside, Simon," he said. "I believe you can see as much as you need to see from the doorway." He picked up an electric torch from the floor beside the door. "Use this."

It might sound childish, I know, but ever since I first encountered Nancy Drew at the age of nine or ten, I've been fascinated by secret passages and the like. How thrilling it was to investigate the old Turnbull mansion with Nancy, and shiver as she found her way through the hidden staircase.

Thus it was with great anticipation that I stepped to the doorway, pushed it further open with my elbow, clicked on the electric torch, and shone it inside. Perhaps I was doomed to disappointment, for I had imagined something a bit grander, more mysterious, than what the light revealed.

To my left, a steep wooden staircase led up to the bedroom above. Here and there, as I waved the electric torch around, I spotted a cobweb, but I could see that someone had indeed swept much of the dust away from the stairs. The air was a bit cooler inside the passage, despite the fact that the doorway had been standing slightly open for quite some time.

I shone the light up the stairs again. From my vantage point I estimated that the steps were almost wide enough to allow two thin persons to walk abreast up or down. The steps appeared more worn in the center. At some point in the past they must have had quite regular use. Perhaps in the days when Giles's grandmother was having her fling with the groom. I grinned.

I stepped away from the door and blinked in the brighter

light of the drawing room. "Where is the entrance to the cellar, Giles?"

"There should be a trapdoor," Giles said. "There's no ring or anything to grab any longer. I believe my grandfather had the opening mechanism removed and the stones replaced. That's why I doubt anyone has made use of it since that time. Deuced difficult to open, I should think."

Robin took the electric torch from me and moved to shine it on the floor. There was an expanse of about six or seven feet square of rough-hewn stone at the bottom of the stairs. I crowded behind Robin and peered over his shoulder. He stiffened when he felt my hand on his shoulder, and I resisted the temptation to squeeze. I wouldn't want him to misinterpret my playful gesture.

"I believe I see it," Robin said, gesturing for me to move back. He snapped off the electric torch and turned to face Giles and me. "It's difficult to tell, with the stone floor, but I believe I see where one of the stones looks a bit less worn. That must be where the original mechanism was."

"How did it work originally?" I asked.

Giles shrugged. "I'm not certain, but I think it must have been some sort of spring mechanism. If you knew precisely where to push, the spring would open the lock, and then you could lift the door up."

The arrival of Robin's SOCO team put an end to further speculation. Giles and I removed ourselves to the library as Robin began to issue instructions. Giles helped himself to another whisky and soda while I made myself comfortable in one of the leather armchairs.

"No, none for me," I said, waving away Giles's offer of a drink.

"Do you really think someone could have gained access to the house through that secret cellar, Simon?" Giles settled himself in his accustomed place behind the desk.

"It's entirely possible," I said. "But that person would

have to have more knowledge of Blitherington Hall than I would have expected. You did tell me, did you not, that the gardener Macleod was quite the crony of your grandfather's?"

"Yes," Giles said. "He would certainly have known of it, because, now that I think about it, I believe he was the one who discovered what was going on between my grandmother and the groom."

"And Macleod had a daughter."

"Jessamy? Good grief, Simon, are you saying that you think Jessamy knew about the secret passage and such?" Giles was thunderstruck. "I never even thought of that."

"I think it's possible, Giles, and we must consider every possibility."

"But what possible motive could she have for killing Zeke Harwood? She had never even met the man."

"As far as we know, Giles, but she might have. You told me that she ran off to London years ago, and she might have known him in her London days."

"That's possible," Giles conceded.

"As for a motive, he did after all humiliate her in front of the village worthies, if you'll remember," I said. "And our Jessamy is rather proud of her position here."

"Well, yes," Giles said, "but that's hardly sufficient motive, don't you think?"

"Probably not, though we shouldn't forget it." I paused, considering another tack. "Tell me, Giles, how difficult is it for someone to get into the main cellar? Can it be done from outside the house?"

Giles considered that for a moment. "There is one way, but whoever did it would get pretty filthy, I should think, just getting in." He explained that there was one small window, on the south side of the Hall, which opened directly into the cellar. "I shouldn't think, however, that it has been opened in donkey's years. I suppose I should let

Chase know that, however, so he and his men can check it out."

"Yes, they'll need to check it," I said. "But it could all be one big red herring. I have the feeling that we've been overlooking something all along. Perhaps this case isn't really as complicated as it seems."

Chapter Twenty-Five

I sat and brooded in silence while Giles got up and lit the wood already laid in the fireplace. Giles stood warming his hands appreciatively before the fire, once he had it going to his satisfaction. Then he turned and toasted his backside while he watched me.

What had I overlooked? If the alibis of Piers, Moira, and Dittany held up, then Jessamy looked like a stronger possibility as the killer. But why would she have wanted to kill Zeke Harwood? Had she known him during her London days? Even if she had, and he had done something horrible to her, why would she have waited so long to exact revenge?

Opportunity was the most likely answer to that last question. The killer had made use of the peculiarities of Blitherington Hall in order to commit a murder that was proving difficult to solve. I wouldn't have thought Jessamy was that clever, but perhaps she was smarter than I had credited.

If not Jessamy, though, who could be the killer? Maybe it was Thompson, the butler. I stifled a laugh. Maybe Thompson, in a misguided fit of loyalty to Lady Prunella, had used his key, gone into the drawing room, and batted Harwood over the head. All so Harwood would not continue to annoy Thompson's mistress.

I was about to share my latest theory with Giles when a knock sounded at the door.

"Enter," Giles called, and Robin Chase opened the door.

"Any luck, Robin?" I asked.

"It rather depends on what you call luck, Simon," Robin said wearily, crossing the room to stand in front of the fire. "Ah, that's just the ticket. It was bloody cold down in that cellar."

Robin had looked a bit blue in the face when he first came in, not to mention the smears of dust here and there on his suit.

"What did you find, Robin?" I asked.

"Plenty of dirt and cobwebs, not to mention the corpses of numerous insects," Robin said. "I doubt anyone had been in that small chamber for fifty years or more."

"I guess that answers one of our questions," I said. "Did you find the way into the main cellar?"

"Oh, yes," Robin said, "though it took a bit of work. We couldn't open it from within, so we went into the main cellar to investigate. We finally found the door, but Sir Giles was quite correct. It had been made completely inoperable. No one got in that way."

"Back to square one, then," I said, a bit deflated.

"Indeed," Robin said, sounding every bit as weary as he looked.

"I regret that you've had to waste time on such a wild goose chase, Detective Inspector," Giles said.

"No help for it, Sir Giles," Robin replied. "We have to check out any possible lead, no matter how slender. At least now we can rule out something."

"May I offer you something to drink? Whisky and soda? Or some tea?" Giles asked, quite the solicitous host.

"Thank you, but no," Robin said. "The SOCOs are packing up, and soon as they're done, we're calling it a night. But we'll be back in the morning."

"Yes, of course," Giles said. "The sooner this is resolved, the better."

"Good night then, Sir Giles, Simon," Robin said, moving away from the fire toward the door. "If you'll excuse me, I'll just see how the pack-up is going. We'll soon be out of your way . . . for the evening, at least."

"Good night, Robin," I said, overlaid by Giles's own "Good night, Chase."

When the door had closed behind Robin, Giles resumed his stance before the fire. "This is bloody impossible, Simon. I'd like to get these people out of my home, but I suppose I'm stuck with them until this is all resolved."

"Would you mind if I used your phone for a call to London?" I had been only half-listening to Giles, as I pondered my next step in the investigation.

"What? Go ahead, Simon. But why do you want to call someone in London right now?"

I smiled. "I'm in search of information, Giles, and I know just the chap in London who can get it for me. I've made use of his services before, and he's extremely efficient." There was no need to tell Giles that my London researcher was a fellow vampire who just happened to play private detective from time to time.

"Be my guest," Giles said, gesturing toward the phone on his desk.

One of my more useful talents is the ability to remember telephone numbers, even those I seldom used, and I punched in Gosling's number. There was a possibility he might be out on a case, but tonight my luck held. He answered on the third ring.

I identified myself, went through the usual pleasantries, then quickly told Gosling what I wanted. "Righty-ho,

Simon," was all he said. He was phlegmatic, Gosling was. Never said more than was necessary, like one of the laconic private eyes from fiction upon which he modeled himself.

Replacing the receiver in its cradle, I smiled at Giles, who was looking rather puzzled. "Why are you so curious about Jessamy, Simon? And why do you have this chappie checking birth and marriage records?"

"A slender possibility, Giles," I said. "It most likely will come to nothing, but if there's a connection between Jessamy and Zeke Harwood, that could be it."

"You mean she might have been married to him?"

"That, or perhaps she bore a child by him. Either or both, even."

"That's incredibly far-fetched, Simon."

I shrugged. "Yes, but we are rather clutching at straws at the moment, aren't we?"

"Then we must hope that this Gosling fellow finds something useful, mustn't we?" Giles grinned, finally moving away from the fire.

I stood. "Now, Giles, before I head for home, I do have one request. Would you mind going with me up to your bedroom?"

"Why, Simon," Giles laughed, "I thought you'd never ask. I'd be delighted." He reached for my hand.

"That's *not* what I meant, Giles," I said, squeezing his hand before releasing it. "Sorry to dash your hopes, but I have investigating on my mind, nothing else."

"I might have known," Giles said, more mildly than I might have expected. "Very well, then, come along."

I followed him out of the library and up the stairs to the first floor. I trod down the corridor alongside him. "Where are your guests? All in their rooms?"

"As far as I know, yes," Giles said. "Did you want to speak with any of them?"

"No, not now," I said, "but I'd rather that they not see us just now."

Giles shook his head and continued down the hall. About two-thirds of the way down, the corridor turned at a very slight angle. So slight, in fact, that it was barely noticeable. But, if I had figured rightly, the angle was just large enough to affect one's vision, if one were standing near the end of the corridor.

We had reached the door to Giles's bedroom, and he opened it and led the way inside. I stopped just inside the door and laid a hand on Giles's arm. "Now, Giles, tell me. When you and Cliff were together last night, were you here in the bedroom? Or were you in the sitting room next door?"

"We were in the sitting room," Giles said. "That's where I was reading when Cliff came and wanted to talk to me. Why?"

"Then let's go next door, into the sitting room. I'll answer your questions in a moment, I promise."

Giles's sitting room was the last chamber on this side of the corridor, and there was a connecting door between it and his bedroom. We entered the sitting room through this door, and I went to the door that opened into the corridor. Motioning for Giles to join me, I opened the door and stepped just outside, into the corridor.

"Was the lighting in the corridor last night at the same level as now?"

Giles peered around me, into the hall. "Yes, at night, when we have guests, the lights are kept at half-power like this."

"That's what I thought," I said. I stood and gazed down the hall. My eyesight is better than that of most humans, and I can see better in the dark than they can. I focused on the doors on the other side of the corridor, following them down, one by one, until I had reached the final door, near the stairs.

"That last door there, on the other side—that's the door to the master bedroom, isn't it?"

Again, Giles peered around me. "Yes, that's it."

"And the next door after that?"

"That's the bathroom. And the next one is the sitting room. There are connecting doors from the master bedroom to the bathroom to the sitting room."

"Just as I thought."

"And then the next room after that is the room occupied by Mrs. Rhys-Morgan."

"And is there a connecting door between her room and the sitting room?"

"Actually, there is," Giles said, "though usually it's kept locked."

"Tell me," I said, "did Harwood insist that Mrs. Rhys-Morgan be placed in the room next to him? And did he know that the rooms were connected?"

"He did ask that she be next to him," Giles said, after thinking about it for a moment. "He didn't inquire about connecting doors, as far as I'm aware, though he would certainly have discovered their existence pretty quickly."

"Good enough," I said. "Now trade places with me. I want to try a little experiment."

We changed places, and Giles stood in the doorway and faced down the hall, toward the stairs.

"Tell me, in this lighting, if a person were to come out of one of those last two or three rooms, could you be sure which one it was?"

Giles squinted, peering down the hallway. "Possibly," he said. "Why do you ask?"

"Just a theory I'm working on," I said, pulling him back inside the sitting room and closing the door softly behind us. "Do me a favor, Giles. In the morning, when you have a moment to speak with Cliff privately, get him to do what we just did, and ask him the same question. Ask him if he can be certain which door it was he saw Piers Limpley coming out of." I paused. "And make sure no one sees you doing this, and make sure Cliff doesn't tell anyone."

"Ah," Giles said. "I see where you're going with this."

"It's one possibility," I said. "It's not much evidence, unfortunately, but it could be quite suggestive. Call me in the morning as soon as you've had a chance to do as I've asked."

"Will do," Giles said. "Now, Simon, before you go . . ." He pulled me close to him, and I did not resist.

The resulting kiss was quite enjoyable, and I smiled all the way home through the unrelenting rain.

Chapter Twenty-Six

I had much on my mind that evening, not only the murder of Zeke Harwood, but also the machinations of the adversary I had dubbed Nemesis. I had the glimmerings of a solution to the murder, but I still had not decided how to deal with Mrs. Wickham.

I considered the actions of Nemesis in bribing or in some other way suborning Violet Glubb to do the dirty work of switching my pills for duds. What had been the point of this little exercise in revenge? Had she intended to do serious harm?

I thought not. She would have known that, sooner or later, I would have sussed out the fact that something was wrong with the pills and taken steps to correct the problem. Before I had done that, however, I might have found myself in a terribly embarrassing situation. I imagined myself having to explain to Giles or Robin or, heaven forfend, Jessamy Cholmondley-Pease, just why I was endeavoring to bite one of them on the neck.

No, I decided, Nemesis hadn't intended serious harm. Rather, I thought she had aimed to disconcert and embarrass me more than anything else. Had she intended some

Night of the Murder

7:20 P.M.—Moira Rhys-Morgan speaks to Harwood in his room

7:25 P.M.—Piers Limpley speaks to Harwood in his room / Lady Prunella overhears the conversation

7:26 P.M.—Lady Prunella hides in bedroom across the hall

7:28 P.M.—Piers crosses the hall to his room / Harwood goes downstairs to the drawing room

7:32 P.M.—Lady Prunella enters the master bedroom, goes down the secret staircase, and watches Harwood for three to four minutes

7:36 P.M.—Lady Prunella comes out of the secret staircase and confronts Harwood

7:40 P.M.—Dittany Harwood receives phone call from flatmate in London / conversation ends at roughly 7:55 P.M.

7:40 P.M.—Piers Limpley and Moira Rhys-Morgan are together in Mrs. Rhys-Morgan's room until 7:55 P.M.

7:42 P.M.—Lady Prunella leaves Harwood in the drawing room / she is seen by someone who reports this anonymously to the police

7:43 P.M.—Lady Prunella is in the library, drinking brandy / she remains in the library until others join her later

7:55 P.M.—Cliff Weatherstone sees Piers Limpley coming out of Mrs. Rhys-Morgan's room / Cliff has been with Giles in Giles's sitting room

7:58 P.M.—Giles and Cliff Weatherstone arrive in the library

7:59 P.M.—Moira Rhys-Morgan arrives in the library

8:03 P.M.—Dittany Harwood and Piers Limpley arrive in the library

8:08/8:10 P.M.—I arrive at Blitherington Hall and proceed to the library

8:30 P.M.—Giles wonders where Harwood is

kind of permanent damage, she would have chosen something less covert and more decisive.

She had certainly succeeded in disconcerting me. She had also put me on alert. I would be far more vigilant from now on, because I doubted that this would be the only time she attempted to annoy me. Whether she would at some point escalate her campaign into something more serious, I had no way of knowing at the moment. She would bear watching.

In the meantime, though, what would I do to answer what amounted to a practical joke? I thought about it for a moment and then an appropriate response came to me. Not only had Nemesis had my pills switched, she had also, I was convinced, leaked word of my previous adventures in sleuthing to the press.

In that case, turnabout was fair play. She would be no more keen to face the scrutiny of the press than I was, and perhaps the best way to answer her little campaign of embarrassment would be to send the press to her own doorstep.

I smiled again. Yes, that was it. An anonymous tip to several of the leading scandal sheets to the effect that the slain decorator had a secret mistress in Abingdon. That would do it. They would annoy her for a day or two, and the score would be even for the moment.

No doubt she would retaliate at some point in the future, but now that I was on my guard, I would be more prepared to thwart any further attempts on her part.

That decided, I turned my mind back to the murder of Zeke Harwood. I had an idea, rather startling at first, how it was done, and by whom. But before I could hope to prove my theory, I needed to answer several questions. I also thought it might be helpful to map out the events before and after the murder apparently took place. Accordingly, I turned on the computer and began creating a timetable of events.

8:35/8:37 P.M.—drawing room door is opened / body of Harwood is discovered

8:40 P.M.—police are summoned

8:47 P.M.—PC Plodd arrives / DI Chase and DS Harper arrive a few minutes later, followed by the SOCO team

I saved the document, then printed it. I sat at my desk and read through my timetable. It was as accurate as I could make it, though there was one item conspicuous by its absence—the actual murder.

There were two periods of time during which the murder could have taken place. The first was between 7:42 P.M., the time when Lady Prunella had left Harwood alive in the drawing room, and 8:03 P.M., when Dittany Harwood and Piers Limpley had arrived in the library. The second was between 8:03 P.M., the time by which everyone was in the library—excluding me, of course—and 8:35 P.M., when we discovered the body en masse.

If the murder had occurred during the second time period, it meant that someone else had killed Harwood. Jessamy Cholmondley-Pease was a possibility, though we had as yet no known motive for her to have committed murder. Perhaps my chap in London would turn up something useful in that regard.

If, however, the murder had taken place during that first time period, there were several possibilities. Either Dittany Harwood had done it and had somehow rigged an alibi, or Piers Limpley or Moira Rhys-Morgan had done it, one providing an alibi for the other. Or perhaps they had acted together. Any of the three of them could have gone down the secret staircase and sneaked up behind Harwood, striking him on the head.

Dittany and Piers might have done it together as well, I realized. They had arrived in the library together, and no one had seen from whence they had come. They might

have come from the drawing room rather than from upstairs. As I had reasoned earlier, the murderer—or murder-
ers, as the case might be—could have taken the key to the
drawing room from Harwood, let himself or themselves
out of the room, then replaced the key *after* we discovered
the body. In those first confused moments after the discovery, one of them could easily have slipped the key back
into Harwood's pocket under cover of examining the body
for signs of life.

It seemed devilishly convoluted. I wondered how much
of it had been planned beforehand, or if it had all been
spur-of-the-moment, the killer simply making use of the
circumstances that presented themselves. Either way, it took
nerve and daring. Which of the suspects possessed the necessary qualities?

If only the police could determine what the killer had
used as weapons. That was also an odd feature of the case,
that at least two different weapons had been used. I also
had an idea about that, and how the killer might have hidden the weapons. I could have rung Robin then and got
him onto it, but the poor man deserved at least this night's
rest. It could keep until the morning.

Besides, I reflected, by the time I called Robin to share
my idea with him, I might have other information that
could help us zero in on a suspect.

I had not been a patient person when I was alive, and
now that I was dead, I was just as impatient as before. I
hated waiting. I was itching to have this thing resolved, to
see whether I was right about my solution to Harwood's
murder.

It was still too early, however, for Gosling to have dug
up the information I had requested him to find. There
wasn't much I could do until then.

I set aside the timetable and concentrated on my other

problem, my plan for getting back at Nemesis. I turned again to the computer, this time using it to connect to the Internet in order to track down the phone numbers to the scandal sheets I wanted to call.

Within minutes I had the numbers I needed, and I started dialing.

It didn't take long to set my little plan into motion. Disguising my voice by assuming a posh British accent, I spun a lurid tale of sordid weekends of sex and depravity, long enjoyed by Zeke Harwood and the mysterious Mrs. Wickham of Abingdon. I had to "out" Harwood as a straight man playing gay for the sake of publicity, and that took a bit of talking, but by the time I had rung off from the third of the papers I called, I was satisfied that I had convinced them to follow up my lead.

Now I had to wait. I had done all I could for the moment, until I heard back from Gosling and until the rest of the world was up and about again.

I slept for about three hours, the most sleep I usually need in any period of twenty-four hours, then sat back down at the computer to write. Energized by the thought that the case would soon be resolved, I worked happily on the latest opus until about eight-thirty the next morning.

Today was Friday, and Violet Glubb would be reporting for work at Laurel Cottage in half an hour. I went upstairs to dress appropriately for the day. I had to be ready, because I was sure that things would start happening quickly once I heard back from Gosling in London.

A couple of minutes after nine, I heard a knock at the door. I opened it and admitted Violet.

"Good morning, Vi," I said, squinting against the sun. The rain had finally ceased, and we had the promise of a decent fall day. I wouldn't have minded more clouds in the sky, but no doubt they would soon return.

"Morning, Mr. Kayjay. How's tricks this morning?" Vi asked cheerfully, unwinding a gaudy scarf from around her neck, in preparation for removing her coat.

"Funny you should use that word, Vi," I said, regarding her unsmilingly.

"Why, whatever do you mean, Mr. Kayjay?" Vi paused in the act of taking off her coat. "Is summat the matter?"

"Come into the sitting room with me," I said, turning away.

She followed me into the room and sat in the chair I indicated, the uncomfortable one. Perched on the edge of the chair, she watched me, her hands playing with the scarf in her lap. Her eyes grew round as she waited for me to speak, and I purposely held off saying anything for a full minute.

"Tell me, Vi, did Mrs. Wickham pay you to switch my pills? Or did she threaten you in some way?"

Violet went deathly pale and began swallowing convulsively. She couldn't speak for a moment. "Oh, Lord, Mr. Kayjay. I never meant no harm, honest I didn't. Mrs. W., she said she knew you and was just playing a friendly little joke on you. She assured me, she did, that them pills wasn't for anything serious and you wouldn't get sick or nothing like that. Else I wouldn't ha' done it, I never would!"

Her voice had risen steadily in pitch through the last few words, by which time she was wailing away.

I regarded her with some pity. I held no rancor against her, because she had been an unwilling dupe and the damage, such as it was, had been short-lived.

"It's okay, Vi, no real harm done. It wasn't a particularly funny joke, but you still shouldn't have done it."

"No, sir," she said, between sobs.

"It was also a pretty elaborate joke, wasn't it?" I said. "After all, you had to move here from Abingdon. Didn't that all seem a bit strange to you?"

Vi nodded emphatically. "Oh, yes, Mr. Kayjay. It did."
She looked down at her hands, still playing with the scarf.
"But I didn't have much choice, like."

"Why not, Vi? Were you in some kind of trouble?"

She wailed again. It took me several minutes to calm her
down enough to get her to talk without breaking into sobs
after every other word. After that, the sordid little tale was
soon told.

Vi had a liking for pretty things, and when she couldn't
afford something she liked, she simply "adopted" it. Mrs.
Wickham had caught her one evening helping herself to a
valuable Staffordshire figure and after that, Mrs. Wickham
would threaten to turn her over to the police if she didn't
do as Mrs. Wickham asked.

"Right wicked she is, Mr. Kayjay." Her secret out, Vi
now turned indignant. "But what am I to do? Now she'll
shop me to the police for sure."

"I wouldn't worry too much about that for the moment,
Vi," I said kindly. "Mrs. Wickham is going to be a bit busy
for a while, and she won't have time to think about that.
Besides, I'll send her a little note, warning her that if she
should try to bother you again, I'll see to it that she's the
one who gets in trouble, not you."

"Oh, Mr. Kayjay, you are a love, you really are!" She
beamed at me as she wiped away the tears. "You'd do that
for me, even after what I done to you?"

"Yes, Vi, I would," I said. "But you must never have
anything more to do with Mrs. Wickham. And you must
promise me that you'll do your best not to 'adopt' anything that doesn't belong to you. If I catch you at it, you'll
have more to worry about than Mrs. Wickham, I assure
you." I treated her to a rather ferocious smile, and she paled
again.

"Oh, no, sir, I won't, I promise you, on me dear mother's
grave. I'll be good."

I had my doubts about that, because if she were a klep-tomaniac, she wouldn't be able to stop herself. But I figured she had been punished enough, at least for the moment.

"I'll hold you to that, Vi," I said, rising from the sofa. "Now I suppose you had better get on with your work."

"Yes, sir," she said, jumping up happily from her chair. She disappeared in the direction of the kitchen. I supposed I was taking a risk by keeping her on, but better the devil you know, as the saying goes. Vi might yet need protection from Nemesis, and I was in a good position to provide that.

I sauntered back to my office and sat down behind my desk. Staring at the phone, I willed it to ring. It was by now almost nine-thirty, and surely Gosling would be ringing me soon with the results of his researches.

The phone rang.

I grabbed up the receiver. "Hello? Is that you, Gosling?"

"No, Simon," came the response. "It's Robin Chase. And I have some good news. We've found the murder weapons."

Chapter Twenty-Seven

"That is good news indeed, Robin," I said. "I was actually going to call you, because I'd had an idea about the murder weapons. It seems that I needn't have bothered."

Robin laughed. "For once, Simon, I'm delighted to say, I got there ahead of you."

"Oh, piffle, Robin," I said. "Now tell me, what were they?"

"We should have spotted them sooner, I must admit," Robin said. "But with the benefit of more complete information from the postmortem, I was able to work it out."

"Now, Robin, stop teasing and tell me."

"Very well, Simon," he said, and I could hear the smile in his voice. "The two wounds, each made by a different-shaped object, had one thing in common. Each of them left behind a minute amount of black paint and iron flake in the wounds."

"And did you find any iron objects, painted black, in the drawing room?" I asked, already guessing at the answer.

"No, Simon, we did not," Robin said.

Before Robin could continue, I interjected, "Instead, you found two iron objects that had recently been painted red."

An exasperated snort came through the line. "And just when did you figure out that bit, Simon?"

"Sometime last night," I said. "I was going to ring you this morning, Robin, and tell you what I had guessed. But you found them without my help."

"Yes," he said. "But that makes it all the more strange. The killer uses both of these small, but heavy... iron sculptures we'll call them, for want of a better word, kills Harwood, then calmly takes the time to paint them both red before putting them back into position near the fireplace. We've found the can of paint and the brush our chappie most likely used, but I doubt we'll find any useful prints."

"The killer had to act quickly," I said. "Particularly if the murder took place before eight o'clock. If it took place after we had all gathered in the library, he or she would have of course had a bit more time."

"Yes," Robin replied. "The time of death is of no help, since the body was discovered so soon after the murder occurred. The police surgeon can't pinpoint it any further than saying it occurred within an hour before we first arrived on the scene."

"Rather frustrating," I said. "But I believe I have figured out how it was done, and by whom." I told him.

Robin listened in silence to my theory. "That's a bit elaborate, don't you think, Simon?" He was skeptical, but he hadn't offered any better theory of his own.

"Yes, it is," I admitted, "and it hangs on at least two pieces of information. I hope to obtain the answers shortly. If I'm right about what I expect to hear, then I believe I'm right about the whole thing."

"And what is it you're waiting to hear? And from whom?"

"Now, Robin," I said. "I must protect my source. I promise you, once I obtain the information, you will easily be able to verify it, and never mind how I got it. I'll let you know as soon as I can. Shouldn't be long now."

"Very well, Simon," Robin said, but he was not best pleased by my answer. "I shall expect you here at Blitherington Hall within the hour."

"Most likely," I said before ringing off. Robin would be stewing a bit, but I couldn't help that. I couldn't do anything more until I heard from Gosling.

The phone call came about half an hour later. While I waited, none too patiently, I could hear Vi moving about the cottage, humming and cleaning. I was too distracted to try to work while I waited, so I simply sat, staring at the phone.

I snatched up the receiver on the first ring. "Hello?"

"Gosling here," he said. "Found what you wanted. Have a pencil handy?"

I jotted down notes while he talked. First item, Jessamy Cholmondley-Pease, nee Macleod. Thirty-two years ago, when she was just seventeen, Jessamy Macleod had given birth to a child out of wedlock, a daughter. The father was listed as one Hezekiah Harwood. Gosling found a record of a marriage between Jessamy and Zeke three months after the birth of the child. When the daughter—who had been named Desiree—was about two years old, Jessamy had decamped, leaving her child in the care of the father. Gosling had found no record of a divorce.

Desiree, I reckoned, must be Dittany. So Zeke had been her father, not her brother. That explained the gap in age between them. Not to mention Dittany's dark mutterings about "family," with which she had threatened her father.

Jessamy had had no further contact with father or daughter that Gosling had been able to determine. In fact, Jessamy had disappeared, more or less, until she had resurfaced in

Snupperton Mumsley about fifteen years ago. Upon her marriage to Desmond Cholmondley-Pease, Jessamy Macleod Harwood had assumed a more socially advantageous position, particularly when her new husband's political star began to rise.

A charge of bigamy, however, could tarnish that star. Jessamy did have, after all, a good motive for murder.

But had she actually done it?

"Thanks, Paul," I said. "You've done well, not that I expected anything less. But I do need one further bit of information, if you could oblige."

"Not a problem, Simon," he said. "What do you need?"

"A phone number," I said. "I fear it may be ex-directory, however."

Gosling laughed. "Piece of cake. Whose number you want?"

"I need the number of the flat of one Dittany Harwood, in London."

"Hang on a tic," Gosling said, and he set the receiver down. After a moment, I heard the rustling of pages before he picked up the phone again. "You're right, Simon. I'll have to make a quick call, if you'll hold."

"Certainly," I said, and I waited.

Within three minutes, Gosling was back on the line. "Called a bloke I know, and he gave me the number."

I jotted it down. "Thanks, Paul. Just send me a bill, per usual."

"Will do, Simon," he said and rang off.

Useful chap, Gosling, as well as discreet; he always seemed able to find out what I needed, and he never asked questions.

I picked up the receiver again and punched in the number Gosling had given me. After two rings, I heard a voice on the other end. Smiling, I hung up the receiver without saying anything.

Bingo. I was right.

Now I knew how it had been done and probably why. Time to head for Blitherington Hall. I picked up the paper with Dittany Harwood's phone number on it and slipped it into my jacket pocket along with my notes from Gosling's researches.

"Vi," I called. "Where are you?"

After a moment she appeared from the kitchen. "Just having a spot of tea, Mr. Kayjay. Is there summat you wanted?"

"Just to let you know that I'll be going out for a while," I said, pulling on my gloves and picking up my hat and sunglasses from the hall table. "Should anyone call, you have no idea where I've gone. Particularly if any member of the press should call or come to the front door." I figured the press would be too busy haring off to Abingdon or camping out at Blitherington Hall to show up at Laurel Cottage, but you never knew.

"Right, Mr. Kayjay. I'll keep mum, never you fear." Her smile was pathetically grateful.

"There's a good girl, Vi," I said. "If I'm not back by the time you've finished, just let yourself out the front door. It will latch behind you."

Outside the sun still shone brightly, though clouds seemed to be moving in. Whistling merrily, I headed the Jag in the direction of Blitherington Hall. This would all soon be over, and Snupperton Mumsley would be all abuzz with Detective Inspector Chase's clever solution to the murder of Zeke Harwood. I intended, as usual, to remain in the background, as far as the public were concerned.

The press cadre were at about half-strength in the lane leading to Blitherington Hall. I smiled. Even now, some of them must be on Mrs. Wickham's doorstep in Abingdon, hopefully playing merry hell with her existence there. One good turn deserves another, after all.

Thompson answered my ring right away. No doubt Robin had told him to expect me.

"Good morning, Thompson," I said, handing off my hat and gloves and tucking my sunglasses into my jacket. "Is Sir Giles about anywhere?"

"Yes, Professor," he said, "but the detective inspector did say as he wanted to see you straightaway you arrived, sir. Begging your pardon."

"I'll see him as soon as I've spoken with Sir Giles," I assured him. "It won't take but a moment, but I must ask Sir Giles something first."

"Very good, sir," Thompson said. "You'll find Sir Giles in his sitting room, I believe."

"Thank you, Thompson," I said. I made haste for the stairs, because I wanted to be out of the way should Robin come looking for me.

Moments later, I knocked on the door to Giles's sitting room. Obeying the command to enter, I walked into the room.

"Morning, Giles," I said. "And how are you this morning?"

"You seem rather chipper this morning, Simon," Giles said, coming forward to greet me with a kiss. "I take it that you have this bally thing worked out?"

"Oh yes," I said. "It will soon be over."

"Would you mind telling me who did it?"

"In a moment, Giles," I said, seating myself in a chair across from him. "But first, were you able to ask Cliff what I wanted?"

Giles nodded. "Yes, Simon, I was. I believe you'll be pleased with his answer. He said he couldn't be entirely certain which door Limpley had come out of. It could have been either the door to Mrs. Rhys-Morgan's room or the door of Harwood's bathroom or sitting room. At that distance, and in that light, he couldn't be positive. He had just assumed it was Mrs. Rhys-Morgan's door, because afterward he had heard Limpley say he had been with Mrs. Rhys-Morgan."

"Good enough," I said. "Now, to answer your question."

Giles sat with admirable patience as I ran through my explanation, which took a few minutes.

"That's beastly complicated," he said, his eyebrows knitted together in a frown of concentration. "Are you sure?"

"Pretty much," I said. "I know it's complicated, but I believe that's what happened. It does sound like something out of a 1930s mystery novel, doesn't it?"

Giles laughed. "It most assuredly does. But if you say that's what happened, Simon, then I believe it must be true."

"Now to prove it," I said, "and there's the rub."

"You should be able to prove parts of it," Giles said, "and if those parts are provable, then the rest must surely follow."

"I think so," I said. "But we'll see. Now I must talk to Robin and tell him everything I've just told you."

"Then what?" Giles said.

"Then, I think," I said, smiling, "we must gather the suspects in the library, where All Will Be Revealed."

Chapter Twenty-Eight

Giles and I proceeded downstairs to the library, where Robin and his sergeant, Harper, were discussing the case and waiting rather impatiently for my arrival.

"Hello, Robin, Sergeant Harper," I said. "Sorry to delay you, but I had one more bit of information to collect before I joined you."

"And what was that, if I might be so bold as to ask?"

Robin was a mite testy, but I couldn't really blame him. I felt a bit like Lord Peter Wimsey making the police dance to his tune.

"Just this," I said, then explained what Giles had learned, on my behalf, from Cliff Weatherstone.

"That does help, I suppose," Robin said, though his tone was doubtful.

"It will, you'll see," I said, "but I think you'll find this a bit more solid." I pulled my notes from my pocket and informed him of the connection between Jessamy Cholmondley-Pease and Zeke Harwood.

"Well, I never," Harper was moved to comment. Robin shot him an admonishing glance.

"Very damaging, Simon," Robin said.

"Oh yes, and it will be quite embarrassing for the fair Jessamy when this gets about. She won't be able to hold her head up in the village after this."

"That might be the least of her worries," Robin said, grim-faced.

"Perhaps," I said. "Now, Robin, do you have your mobile with you?"

Puzzled, Robin reached into a pocket and withdrew his phone. "Yes, why?"

"Be so good as to call this number," I said. "It's the number to Dittany Harwood's flat in London."

Robin forbore to assert that I had gone completely round the bend. Instead, he complied with my command. In a moment, someone answered at the other end. He was so startled he almost dropped the phone.

"Um, no, Thompson, thank you," Robin said. "I believe I dialed this number by mistake." He ended the call and tucked the mobile back into his pocket.

"Quite clever, wasn't it?" I said. "It's called something like Call Divert, I believe. We call it call forwarding in the States. Very handy when one's going to be away from the home phone for a while and one doesn't want to miss any calls. I smiled. "Or if one wants to set up a fake alibi."

"So much for her alibi, then," Robin said. "Now I begin to see what you've been getting at, Simon."

I smiled modestly. "Thank you, Robin. Of course, all this still remains to be proven. I have an idea about that, if you'll play along, that is."

Robin drew in a deep breath, as if anticipating bad news. "And what, pray tell, is this idea of yours?"

"Since I've been playing Miss Marple to your Inspector Craddock,"—Robin winced and did his best not to look in Harper's direction—"or, if you will my Poirot to your Japp, why not take it a step further? Assemble all the suspects here in the library, and let me have at them."

Harper could no longer restrain himself. He shook with mirth, and nothing Robin said could quell him, for at least five minutes.

"Be quiet, man," Robin said finally, in complete exasperation. "This whole thing is bloody ridiculous, a right farce. Do you know what would happen to my career if this got out?"

"Now, Robin," I said soothingly, "I'm sure Detective Sergeant Harper wouldn't tell tales out of school. And once it's over, and you've got the case wrapped, I doubt your superiors will care. This will look like a brilliant success for you. I assure you, I intend to take no credit for this. It's all yours for the asking."

Harper had at last managed to control himself, and Robin stared thoughtfully into space for a long moment, while Giles and I waited in silence.

"Very well," Robin said. "It seems the most expedient way to get everything out in the open. Either Harper and I spend hours questioning all the suspects, trying once more to break them down, or we give this idea of yours a go."

"I don't think you'll be sorry," I said. "Now all we need to do is get everyone here, into the library. Will you call Jessamy Cholmondley-Pease and get her here? I assume the others are easy to round up."

Robin reached for the phone. Jessamy was at home, and though she protested at first, she eventually agreed that she would present herself at Blitherington Hall within the half hour.

Next, Giles summoned Thompson and asked him to inform his guests that Detective Inspector Chase required their presence in the library within the half hour.

"Very well, Sir Giles," Thompson said.

While we waited, Harper and I arranged chairs for all the suspects. Harper, when the time approached, stationed himself near the door, the only exit from the room, in readiness, should he have to prevent someone from attempting to leave.

"A point of procedure, Robin," I said, as if struck by a sudden thought. "How shall we do this? What do you think best?"

"Oh, give over, Simon," Robin said. "I suppose I should speak first, tell them I expect their full cooperation and all that, then turn it over to you."

"Thank you, Robin," I said. "It really is very good of you."

Giles had a word with his mother, whom he summoned to the library ahead of the rest. He explained the situation to her and impressed upon her that she must not speak unless called upon. She agreed, quite meekly for her.

A knock at the door heralded the first arrival, and within five minutes they had all assembled and seated themselves in the chairs provided. I stood to one side and watched as Robin greeted each of them. I could sense heightened pulse rates, but none of them seemed frightened—with the possible exception of Jessamy, the last to arrive. She collapsed into a chair and gazed about, as if disoriented.

"Good morning, ladies and gentlemen," Robin said. "Thank you for all complying so promptly with my request. We have new information that will, I believe, allow us to wrap up this case quite quickly. But there are some items remaining that need to be cleared up. I've asked you all to be here together so that we may do this as a group." He turned and indicated me. "Professor Kirby-Jones has kindly agreed to assist me by taking us through the evidence. I would ask that you all listen attentively, and if he asks a question, to answer truthfully."

He stepped aside, and I took his place in front of Giles's desk, facing the assembled group.

"Thank you, Detective Inspector," I said, beaming at them all as if I were addressing a group of new students.

"We shall proceed forthwith, and I must ask you to bear with me as I go along. As Detective Inspector Chase said, there are some items we must address and try to clear up, so that we may see the picture more clearly."

No one made any verbal response to this, though Jessamy continued to twitch about in her seat, as if she found it somehow painful. The others regarded me passively, Cliff Weatherstone being the only one to exhibit any vestige of interest in what was about to take place.

"Very well, then," I said. "Let us start with motives, then. There must be a motive for any crime, however trivial. Harwood was not a particularly likeable chap, at least in my observation, but mere dislike is not usually a motive for murder." I paused to strike a reflective pose. "No, it must have been something stronger.

"To begin, let us take the case of Cliff Weatherstone."

Cliff jerked upright in his chair, and Dittany Harwood turned to examine him with slitted eyes.

"Cliff has very successfully, and for a number of years, directed the victim's television program, 'Très Zeke.' Yet, I discovered, Harwood was on the point of dispensing with Cliff's services when he left England for the States. While he went off, no doubt, to further fame and fortune in America, Cliff was going to be left behind, perhaps disgraced and looking for a new job."

Cliff shot me a look of active dislike. I merely smiled.

"It was through Cliff I discovered that, contrary to the image Harwood had created, our late unlamented was not, in fact, gay, and his unwelcome attentions to his handsome producer were nothing more than an act. An act which, over time, became increasingly difficult to bear, and that, coupled with the fact that he was about to be fired, might have made anyone long for revenge."

"I didn't kill him!" Cliff could no longer restrain himself. He popped up from his seat and waved one arm about. "He was a bloody bastard, and I hated him, but I didn't kill him."

"I don't believe I said that you did," I observed mildly. "Do sit down again, there's a good chap."

Cliff subsided into his chair.

"Thank you. No, I said you might have longed for revenge. Tell me, Cliff, it was you, wasn't it, who hired the chap to throw paint on Harwood at the book signing?"

Cliff's mouth opened and closed, then he found the ability to speak. "Yes, I arranged that stunt, but I didn't kill him."

"I shall repeat myself," I said. "I didn't say you killed him. But you did manage to annoy and embarrass him, didn't you? And had not someone else stepped in and killed him, no doubt you would have continued your campaign of irritation."

Cliff clamped his mouth shut and said not another word.

"Just as I thought," I said. "We're after someone who's more bite than bark." Cliff glowered at me. "Now let us turn to the next person on our list. Jessamy Cholmondley-Pease."

"Me?" Jessamy squeaked. "I didn't kill him. I didn't even know him, except from the telly."

"Now, Jessamy, you know that's not true," I said in pitying tones. "As much as it pains me, I'm afraid I must reveal your past in front of these people." I shook my head. "Though I suspect, of course, that it was no secret to most of them."

"What do you mean?" Moira Rhys-Morgan demanded. "I'd never seen this woman before we came to this godforsaken house."

"No, I doubt you had, but surely Zeke must have told

you about his wife? After all, that's one of the reasons he couldn't make an honest woman of you. That and the fact that he had convinced his public he was gay."

Moira paled, sitting as still as if she had turned to stone. No one else said a word.

"Yes, poor Jessamy, I'm afraid we've discovered that you were still legally married to Harwood. I wonder, does Desmond know about any of this?"

Gasping for breath, Jessamy shook her head.

"He'll know soon enough," I said. "I wonder how he'll react when he discovers that he wasn't really married to you all these years? And, moreover, that you have a grown daughter you probably haven't seen in almost thirty years?"

Jessamy turned to look at Dittany, christened Desiree, but Dittany steadfastly refused to look at her mother.

"Oh, it's all true," Jessamy wailed, facing me once again. "He was an 'orrible man, Zeke was, and I never should've left the poor tyke with him. I can't blame her for not speaking to me. But it wasn't me what killed him. I swear it!" Her accent had completely deteriorated under stress.

"But you must have wanted him dead," I said. "Particularly when he turned up here. You must have been quite worried, as soon as Lady Prunella had announced it in the village, that once he was here, Zeke might let it slip to your so-called husband."

"He, he threatened me," Jessamy said between sobs, "but he were just playing with me. He liked being nasty, the bloody bastard. He couldn't afford for anyone to know he was married to me, neither, but he was being bloody-minded anyway."

"Yes, I think we can all agree that he was quite a nasty man, in many ways. But before we proceed further, you must answer one question for me, Jessamy. I want you to think back to the time in London, before you left Zeke. Did you ever tell him about the secret stairway here at Blitherington Hall? How it worked, where it was, and all that?"

Jessamy stared at me, puzzled. I could almost see the tiny gears in her brain grinding away. "Oh, then that's how—" she clamped a hand over her mouth and stared at me with frightened eyes.

"How what, Jessamy?" I said. "What were you going to say?"

Tears were streaming down her face. "Please don't make me answer that, please don't."

"I'm afraid you must," Robin Chase said, gently. "You can't hold anything back now, Mrs. Cholmondley-Pease."

It took her a moment to get her sobbing under control, but at last Jessamy spoke. "I did tell Zeke about it, back in London. He liked hearing about such a grand house and all the little secrets such a posh family had. I never thought nothing about it, because I never planned on coming back to this village. And I never expected Zeke to show up here, neither."

"Did you ever make use of the staircase yourself these past few days, Jessamy?"

Her eyes grew wide. "Yes, I did, just once."

"When was that?" I asked.

"That afternoon," she said. "Before Zeke was killed. I had been trying to catch him alone, but he was always busy. I kept watching from the hallway, and when I saw everyone else leaving the drawing room for a break, Zeke didn't come out. I knew he wouldn't let me in the drawing room, so I nipped upstairs and sneaked in the bedroom. No one saw me. I thought they had all gone outside or into the dining room for tea."

"And did you talk to Zeke?"

She nodded. "He was just as nasty as I expected, but I

told him if he said anything about him and me still being married, it would embarrass him as much as me."

"Did he seem surprised when you popped out of the wall like that?"

"No," Jessamy said. "He'd remembered about the secret stairs, he said, and he had already used them a couple of times himself. It was why he kicked up such a fuss about which bedroom he wanted. He wanted to be sure to have that room, just so he could use those stairs."

"Do you think he told anyone else about them, Jessamy?"

"No, he didn't," Jessamy said. "He didn't want them to know, in case he wanted to spy on them while they was working and they thought he wasn't around."

That could be a problem.

"Are you sure about that, Jessamy? Think very carefully."

Her face crumpled, and she began to cry again.

"What is it, Jessamy? You must tell us, you know."

Jessamy sobbed some more, then thrust out her hand, pointing. "She knew. Oh, God forgive me, she knew. She saw me coming out of the wall in Zeke's bedroom."

She was pointing at her daughter, Dittany.

Chapter Twenty-Nine

While Jessamy mumbled "I'm sorry" over and over, like a mantra, Dittany steadfastly ignored her.

"Ah, yes, Dittany," I said, turning to face that young woman directly. "Or should I say, Desiree? After all, that was the name you were christened with, wasn't it?"

"It's no use, you can't stick me with this," she said coolly, ignoring my jibe about her name. "I have an alibi, and so do Piers and Moira." She jerked her head in the direction of her mother. "That's who you want, right there. I'll bet *she's* got no alibi."

Jessamy cried all the harder at this accusation, though what she expected from a daughter she had abandoned so long ago, I had no idea.

"True, I doubt Jessamy has an alibi for the time of the murder," I said agreeably. "The murder had already taken place by the time you, Piers, and Moira joined Sir Giles and Lady Prunella in the library. And I'm afraid, Miss Harwood, that you have no alibi after all."

"Don't be bloody ridiculous," she said. She was defiant, but beneath that I could feel the first real stirring of fear.

"Tell me, Miss Harwood, do you recognize this telephone number?" I recited the digits of her home number to the room.

Dittany's eyes narrowed. "Yes," she said, "that's my number. It's ex-directory, though. How did you get it?"

I ignored her question. "What do you think would happen, Miss Harwood, if I asked Detective Inspector to take out his mobile and call your number? Would the phone ring in your flat?"

She did not answer.

"Or would it, Miss Harwood, ring here at Blitherington Hall? Shall we put it to the test?"

"There's no need," she said.

"Then you will admit that you used Call Divert to have your phone calls forwarded here to Blitherington Hall?"

Her head snapped up at that. "It wasn't I who did that, you fool! It was my bloody flatmate, before she left on holiday. She got it all wrong, the silly cow. She was supposed to divert the calls to my mobile."

"Oh, really," I said. "That's an interesting point. If your flatmate hadn't made such a mistake, you might have come up with a better alibi for yourself, one that couldn't be so easily broken."

She glowered at me as I strode back and forth in front of the group. "You see, this is how I believe it was done. Once Miss Harwood realized the mistake her flatmate had made, she decided to put the mistake to good use in her alibi. This way, she could use her mobile, call her flat in London, and the call would be diverted back to Blitherington Hall. Disguising her voice, she would ask to be put through to Miss Harwood, and once the call was put through to her room, she could leave the mobile on and the extension in her room off the hook while she proceeded with the rest of the plan. When she was done, she came back to the room, ended the call, and finished getting ready to join everyone downstairs in the library."

I beamed at them. "Quite clever, wasn't it? The police had already confirmed that such a call had been put through to her room here at Blitherington Hall, but eventually, I'm afraid, they would have discovered that the call had originated with your mobile, Miss Harwood, if they had dug that deep. And I'm quite certain that they would have."

She regarded me in stony silence. Jessamy stared at her daughter in horror, her worst fears confirmed. Tears continued to stream down, but at least she no longer sobbed loudly.

"And so, there you have it," I said. "Once Miss Harwood had established the phone connection she would use as her alibi, she could nip down the hall to her father's room, let herself in, sneak down the secret staircase, then surprise her father in the drawing room.

"There was, however, quite a lot to do to pull this off. She had to strike her father over the head, not once, but several times, and she also used two different blunt objects. That was rather an odd fact, I thought. She then had to arrange her father on the sofa where we found him and dab him about with the red paint. Moreover, she had to go up and down the secret stairs with a drop cloth to erase any footprints, or so she hoped. Finally, she had to cover the two murder weapons with that same red paint and hope not to get any telltale paint on herself."

I paused and regarded my audience. Dittany was watching me warily, unsure of whether to speak and risk giving something away. Piers shifted uneasily in his chair, but Moira remained still and stone-faced.

"Yes, there was quite a lot to do, even though, if I've calculated correctly, Dittany had about twenty minutes in which to do it. She could have already been hiding behind the panel in the drawing room while Lady Prunella was arguing with Harwood. In fact, I wouldn't be surprised if she were the one who made the anonymous call to the police to inform them of the time Lady Prunella left the drawing room. I had thought it was Jessamy, but I think it more likely it was Dittany."

She squirmed a bit at that but still refused to speak.

"Even if Dittany were already behind the panel and popped out as soon as Lady Prunella left, she still had quite a lot to accomplish before she had to be back upstairs to get ready for dinner. It's just possible, but I don't think that's quite the way it happened."

"But that must be it, Simon!" Lady Prunella could contain herself no longer and hopped up out of her chair. "I say, well done, Simon. You've solved it."

"Thank you, Lady Prunella, but I'm afraid your kudos are a trifle premature."

Crestfallen and confused, she sank back into her seat.

"You see," I said confidingly, as if I were speaking to Lady Prunella alone, "Dittany did not act alone."

"Oh, come off it, man," Piers spoke up, attempting a skeptical tone and failing miserably. "I mean to say, who would have helped her do such a thing?"

"Really, Mr. Limpley, were you going to sit there and let Dittany take sole blame for the murder? It's not the gentlemanly thing to do. And you don't seriously believe that she wouldn't shop you, and Mrs. Rhys-Morgan, the minute she got the chance?"

"You can leave my name out of this," Moira said hotly. "I had nothing to do with this."

"I do wish I could believe that, Mrs. Rhys-Morgan," I said. "But I'm afraid it won't wash. I don't believe you actually struck one of the blows, but you were there, and you helped, probably by applying the paint to the corpse, or by painting the murder weapons with the red paint after they had been used. I'm not sure which, but I've no doubt you were involved."

Moira did not attempt any further denials.

"I kept wondering, you see, why two different weapons were used. The killer might have tried with one weapon, found it unsatisfactory, then picked up another. But that seemed rather sloppy, given the other details. That was what made me wonder whether more than one person was involved. As soon as I thought of that, I began to see how it might have been done."

I faced Piers Limpley and pointed an accusing finger at him. "It was you, Limpley, and Miss Harwood who struck the actual blows, wasn't it? Come now, admit it. You wouldn't want Mrs. Rhys-Morgan to take the blame for something she didn't do."

I had counted on his affection for Moira to play upon his chivalric instincts, and he did not let me down.

"Moira didn't strike him," Piers said in considerable agitation. "Dittany and I did. It was just as you said. Moira helped us, but she didn't kill him." He began to sob. Moira reached over to stroke his arm.

"You bloody fool," Dittany hissed.

"Tell me, Miss Harwood, did you plan to murder your father before you came to Blitherington Hall? Or did you simply seize the moment, once you found out about the secret staircase and realized its possibilities?"

Dittany just sat and glared at me.

"Yes, well," I said. "Either way, it was premeditated. I've no idea how the courts here treat that, but it will be a significant point for the prosecution, no doubt.

"Moving on, then. With the three of them acting in concert the whole episode worked much more easily. They could accomplish everything and still get back upstairs in time to be seen coming downstairs to the library, if necessary. Mr. Limpley was even seen in the upstairs hall, ostensibly coming out of Mrs. Rhys-Morgan's room. The witness, Mr. Weatherstone, has confirmed, however, that Mr. Limpley could just as well have been coming out of one of the other doors a bit farther down the hall."

I paused, shaking my head as if in admiration. "It was a bold and daring plan, and it took great nerve. If anyone had seen you darting about in the hallway upstairs, that would have put an end to it, very quickly. But luck was with you, for a time at least."

Robin stepped forward, about to proceed with the arrests, but I held up my hand.

"I just thought of one more thing; a small loose thread, if you will." I had almost forgotten it, I had been so hot on the chase. "The drop cloth you used to remove the dust from the secret stairs. It was found in the drawing room. Of course it had to be left there, but if you used the stairs *after* you used the drop cloth, you ran a greater risk of leaving some kind of evidence behind. Tell me, Mrs. Rhys-Morgan, it was you, wasn't it, who came back down the stairs with the drop cloth after Miss Harwood and Mr. Limpley went up the stairs to their rooms? And then you waited until the right time, took the key from Mr. Harwood's pocket, let yourself out of the drawing room, locked it behind you, and proceeded calmly to the library. Later on, when we discovered the body, you slipped the key back into his pocket."

I nodded my head admiringly. "That was quite a nice touch, actually, all of you rushing forward like that to render aid to a man you all knew was already dead. That way you could explain it later to the police if you just happened to have any red paint on your bodies or your clothes. Very clever, very clever indeed."

This time when Robin stepped forward to begin the process of arresting them for the murder of Zeke Harwood, I did not stop him. When the formalities were concluded, Robin and Sergeant Harper escorted them out of the library.

"I think brandy all round might be a good idea, if you don't mind, Giles," I said, and he moved quickly to comply with my request. I assisted him in passing round the glasses, and Jessamy downed hers in a single gulp. My, that must have burned, but at least it brought some color back to her ravaged face.

Lady Prunella was uncharacteristically silent. I could see her sitting there, mentally working through it all as she sipped at her brandy. It might take her awhile, but eventually she would have it all sorted out.

Cliff Weatherstone came to me with grudging admiration in his eyes. "Damned if Giles wasn't right, Simon. You did get it all sorted out. And what an unholy mess it all was, too."

"Thank you, Cliff," I said. "It was rather complicated, but the police were bound to figure it out sooner or later. I just helped them get there sooner."

Cliff laughed. "I'm just pleased it's not my neck in a noose." He sipped his brandy. "I'd never have thought Piers had it in him. Dittany, yes, she was always a deep one. To think she was that creep's daughter! And Moira, too. I was quite shocked at that."

"They must all have hated him quite terribly," Giles said, frowning. "He was extremely unpleasant, but to have people hate you that much. That's horrible."

"Yes, it is," Jessamy spoke up. "But Zeke was like that. He took what he wanted, and be damned to the rest of us. I'll never forgive myself for leaving that poor child with him."

None of us could think of a response to that.

"I believe the police will find," I said, to cover the awkward pause that had ensued, "Harwood was planning to leave them all behind when he went to America. I doubt he wanted to be encumbered with any of them, and not just you, Cliff."

"Bloody bastard," Cliff said. "Frankly, I can't say that I blame them for what they did."

"If you'll all excuse me," Jessamy said, "I think I'll be going home." She got shakily to her feet and stood there, looking quite forlorn.

I wondered whether someone should offer to drive her home, for her own safety, and to my surprise, Cliff Weatherstone offered to do just that. In grateful surprise, Jessamy accepted his offer.

"And then I think I'll stop in the village for a few pints," Cliff said as he followed Jessamy out the door of the library. "If anyone wants to join me, that's where you'll find me."

"I shall be so *terribly* glad when these people are gone from my home," Lady Prunella announced. "But *whatever* are we to do about the drawing room, Giles?"

Giles sighed and set down his brandy snifter. Over his mother's head, he caught my eye and smiled. "I rather think, Mummy, that we'll have to have the decorators in."

I will never repeat the word that Lady Prunella uttered then. Dead I may be, but I am a gentleman still.